Love Released
Book Two Of Women Of Courage
Love Released Serial
By
Geri Foster

Thank You

Dear Reader,

Thank you for reading *Book One of Women of Courage, Love Released*. I know venues are filled with many authors and books and the choices are limitless. I'm flattered that you choose my book. There are additional books in this series and if you enjoyed Cora and Virgil's journey, I hope you'll read the others.

If you'd like to learn when I publish new books, please sign up for my **Newsletter** www.eepurl.com/Rr31H. Again, I appreciate your interest and I hope you'll check out my other books.

Sincerely,

Geri Foster

Visit me at:

www.facebook.com/gerifoster1

www.gerifoster.com/authorgerifoster

www.gerifoster.com

Join us for discussion of Women of Courage@

https://www.facebook.com/groups/689411244511805/

Love Released
By Geri Foster

First Edition

Copyright 2015 by Geri Foster

ISBN-13: 978-1511762281

ISBN-10: 1511762284

Cover Graphics
Kim Killion
Lilburn Smith

All rights reserved. Without limiting the rights under copyright reserved above, no part of this publication may be reproduced, stored in or introduced into a retrieval system or transmitted in any form or by any means (electronic, mechanical, photocopying, recording, or otherwise) without the prior written permission of both the copyright owner and the above publisher of this book.

Author contact information: geri.foster@att.net

This is a work of fiction. Names, characters, places, and incidents are either the product of the author's imagination or are used fictitiously. Any resemblance to actual persons living or dead, businesses, events, or locales is purely coincidental.

GERI FOSTER

ACKNOWLEDGEMENTS

This book dedicated to my husband, Laurence Foster. After all these years you're still my one and only love. Thank you for your support, and for believing in me when I had doubts. You've shown me that dreams really do come true and love isn't just in romance novels.
Always,
Geri Foster

LOVE RELEASED

CHAPTER ONE

Cora Williams and her nephew, Jack, had ridden with Sheriff Virgil Carter to Joplin and later stopped for lunch before returning back to Gibbs City, Missouri. When they pulled to the curb outside of her house, she noticed the door stood open. Thinking it was her friend JJ in the house, Cora wasn't concerned until she noticed the new steps.

"Virgil." She turned to him. "The door is wide open."

He came around the car and touched her arm. "You and Jack stay right here."

"Pal," Jack called. "Pal, where are you?"

Cora had a feeling this wasn't going to end well. Who would break into her home? What did they expect to find? Wringing her hands with worry, she watched as Virgil slowly shoved the door of her home wider and called out.

"This is Sheriff Carter. Anyone in here?"

She grabbed her nephew by the shoulder. "Jack, stay here by me."

"But where's Pal?" Tears gathered in his deep, blue eyes. "What if he's hurt or even dead?"

"The sheriff will find him. In the meantime stay here and wait."

Cora left Jack and moved to the yard. Maggie ran across the street to meet her. "What's going on at your house?"

"I don't know." She clutched Maggie's arm. "When we pulled up, the door was open."

"Briggs heard the dog barking like crazy earlier. He looked out the window but didn't see anything unusual."

"Pal isn't answering."

Virgil disappeared into the interior of the house. Maggie gripped her hand and they waited for what seemed an entire day before Virgil walked out carrying the dog.

Jack broke into a run. "Pal, Pal, are you okay?"

The little terrier was so weak he couldn't move his head. Virgil cradled him against his chest.

He looked at Cora. "He's been hurt. Probably kicked or something like that."

Cora grabbed Jack by the shoulder to stop him. "Sit down and Virgil will put Pal in your lap. Be real still."

Swiping away tears, Jack sat on the porch and held out his hands. "Is he gonna be okay, Virgil?"

Virgil gently laid Pal in Jack's outstretched arms. "We'll have to wait and see."

"Why is there blood on his mouth?"

"It looks like he bit someone so hard he lost a tooth."

Cora ran inside and grabbed an old sheet. Back on the porch she pressed around the dog's ribs and he yelped.

Jack clutched Pal to his chest. "Don't hurt him, Aunt Cora."

Virgil was right. Someone had kicked Pal hard enough to break his ribs. She worried about internal injuries. If something was punctured or severely injured, she wouldn't be able to save him.

As tears ran down Jack's cheeks, she touched his shoulder. "He's a very brave dog. I'm going to wrap him up. That will make him more comfortable."

"Will it hurt?"

"Not once it's done."

Jack buried his face in Pal's fur. "I love him so much."

She pushed back the young boy's hair. "I know you do. That's why I want you let Virgil hold him."

Cradling his pet, Jack turned away to shield the dog from the others. "No, no I won't. He's my dog and I don't want you hurting him."

Virgil sat beside Jack. "Let me hold him while your aunt fixes him up."

"But I want to keep him."

Reaching down, Virgil gently took Pal from Jack's arms. "I'll give him right back. I promise."

Cora worked as fast as she could to get the bandages around Pal's middle. It had to be snug, but if she made it too tight, his lungs wouldn't be able to expand.

Tommy and Ronnie ran into the yard.

Tommy asked, "What's wrong with Pal?"

Ronnie stepped closer. "Is he dead?"

Jack jumped up. "No, he ain't dead. I'll punch you in the nose if you say that again."

Hurt, Ronnie stepped back and lowered his head. "I'm sorry. I don't want anything to happen to him."

While Virgil watched, Cora busily wrapped the trembling dog. "Jack sit back down. Ronnie is your friend and he meant no harm."

"I don't want nobody saying Pal's dead."

Virgil held the dog's head. "I know, son. But saying something doesn't make it true." He glanced at Ronnie. "Your friends love your dog as much as you do. They deserve to be treated better."

Tears rolled down Jack's face. "I'm sorry. I just don't want Pal to die."

"It's okay." Cora finished and wadded up the extra cloth. There wasn't much she could do. He would either make it through the night or he wouldn't. She didn't have the equipment or the skill to mend a dog.

"Let's take him inside so he can rest."

Jack ran ahead and grabbed a blanket.

"Not that one, get the one on the washer."

Coming back with the blanket, Jack spread it out next to his bed. Cora bunched it up so Pal would have some cushioning.

Virgil laid the pup down. "Let's see how he does during the night."

Jack forced a brave face. "Maybe tomorrow he'll be able to run and play."

Cora hugged her nephew. "His injuries won't heal that fast. He needs time. It could take days."

Jack looked up at her, his eyes pleading and wet. "But he will get better, right?"

"I hope so, but we'll see how it goes. Now, let's leave him here to sleep."

"I don't want to leave him alone."

"He needs to rest." She looked down at Pal's exhausted body. "See, he's very weak."

Jack, Tommy and Ronnie left the bedroom with long, miserable faces. Cora glanced at Virgil's tight and drawn features.

As they entered the kitchen she saw Mr. Clevenger making his way across the backyard. Maggie opened the door and allowed him to enter. He held his cane in one hand, his shotgun in the other.

"What in blue blazes is going on over here?"

Virgil took his weapon and put it on the counter, out of the children's reach. "Did you hear any noises?"

"I heard that mutt barking his fool head off."

Jack ran to Mr. Clevenger. "A robber came and Pal scared him off."

"Horse feathers! What are you talking about, boy?"

Virgil moved Jack aside and stood in front of the neighbor. "We just came back from Joplin. The front door was wide open." Virgil propped his hip against the counter. "What did you hear?"

Mr. Clevenger leaned on his cane, his eyes taking in the surroundings. "You know, I've never been in this house."

Cora stepped forward. "Welcome. Come in and sit down. I was just going to put on a pot of coffee."

Virgil, Maggie and Mr. Clevenger sat at the kitchen table. Taking cups from the cupboard, Cora then searched the breadbox for something to snack on. Settling on a cinnamon loaf, she sliced the sweet bread and placed it on a plate.

She went to Jack and his friends. "You boys can sit in there with Pal. But don't touch him and be quiet. He's very nervous. Someone has hurt him and he's scared."

Little Ronnie put his grubby, little finger to his mouth. "We'll be quiet as a little mouse."

She smiled. "That's good boys." She watched as they tiptoed into Jack's bedroom.

Back in the kitchen, she turned down the pot and allowed the coffee to perk. "Mr. Clevenger, did you see anything?"

"Well, I noticed your back door was open and I came over and closed it."

She looked at Virgil. "Do you think the person had left by then?"

"Cora, can you look around to see if anything is missing? Maggie can pour the coffee."

She left the kitchen with Virgil beside her. They entered her bedroom and she glanced uncomfortably at the bed. "It's kind of odd that a burglar would come into the room where I sleep."

"It makes me mad. Just who the hell does this person think he is?"

Walking to her closet, she noticed all her clothes were on the floor with several hangers on top. She wrinkled her brow. "Why would they do that?"

"I don't know." Picking them up, she put her things on the bed and began hanging them back in the closet.

Done with that chore, she opened her dresser and all her underthings were scattered around instead of neatly folded as she kept them.

"You keep your personal things in such disorder?"

"No, I never have."

"Is anything missing?"

Searching frantically, she looked up and their eyes clashed. "I think a couple of pairs of my underwear are gone."

"Anything else?"

"Nothing that I can see."

"I don't think this was a robbery in the true sense that someone came in her looking for valuables."

They returned to the kitchen. Mr. Clevenger sipped his coffee and munched on the cinnamon bread. "Anything missing?"

"Not that we could find."

"Why in tarnation would someone break in and not take anything?"

Virgil leaned down and picked up a piece of brown material peeking out from beneath the couch. "What's this?"

Cora stepped closer. "I've never seen it before."

Maggie looked closely. "Could be that Pal caught a thief and tore that from his trousers or a shirt."

Virgil rubbed the fabric between his fingers. "This is too thick to be a shirt. More like a pair of pants."

Cora went to the kitchen and slumped in the chair. Maggie poured her a cup of coffee then placed her hand on Cora's shoulder. "You get off your feet."

"Who in the world would want to rob me?"

Mr. Clevenger said gruffly, "I think that mutt might've stopped the person from doing what they planned. He was making quite a ruckus."

Virgil took a chair and looked at Mr. Clevenger. "You said the back door was open?"

"Yeah, and I came over and closed it."

"You didn't see anyone?"

"No, but then I didn't think to look. I just figured missy there was so excited to be going to town with such a spiffy looking fella she forgot to shut the door."

Cora lowered her head. "I made sure both doors were shut."

"I'm thinking someone might've come in the back door, but Pal ran him out the front."

Maggie folded her arms. "Briggs and I were outside earlier this morning and we didn't see anything." She shook her head. "I can't imagine anyone bold enough to break into a home in the middle of the day."

"I won't have that happening in my county." Virgil stood. "I'll unload your things then I'm going to my office and get John. We'll canvas the neighborhood and see if we can find anything."

"I'll keep Jack inside."

Virgil glanced in the small bedroom. "I don't think you'll have a problem with that. He won't leave Pal."

CHAPTER TWO

Virgil entered his office and slammed the door so loud, John jumped out of his seat.

"What's wrong?"

"While I took Cora and Jack to Joplin, someone broke into their home."

John's eyes grew wide and disbelief covered his face. "In the middle of the day?"

"Yes."

"Well, I'll be a son of a bitch." John jammed his hat on his head. "Let's find out who did that."

They left in the squad car, slowing when they came to Cora's neighborhood. They cruised the side streets. Few people were out and about this late into the afternoon. Many residents were wrapping up their day and getting ready for supper.

On Main Street, the townspeople went about their business without hesitation. No doubt anxious to get home before dark. They slowly drove by the dry cleaners.

Virgil lowered his head and tried to see inside. "All clear there?"

John fanned his flashlight. "No one there."

They turned the corner, and a sound captured Virgil's attention. He looked behind the cleaners and the small attached shed. "What does Bart keep in there?"

John wrinkled his brow. "Supplies I would suppose."

"I've never been in there. Let's take a look." Virgil backed up the black and white where the headlights shined on the door of the building even though it wasn't completely dark yet.

Virgil watched as John carefully stepped out of the car and pulled his gun. He joined the deputy. They both stared at the door. Virgil kicked the side. "Anyone in there?"

"Come out with your hands up."

"Don't make us shoot you."

Another sound had Virgil cocking his gun. Just as he was about to kick in the door, a yellow and white alley cat slithered out meowing.

John lowered his weapon. "It's just a cat."

Virgil stepped closer. "But we don't know what else."

"You thinking someone might be in there?"

"We don't know until we open it." Virgil kicked in the door, and John shined his flashlight.

"Well, I'll be damned."

They both stepped back and stared. In the wooden shed, no larger than an eight by eight, bottles of bootleg whiskey had been stacked from floor to ceiling. Virgil guessed there had to be several thousand dollars' worth of illegal liquor.

Virgil looked at John. "Bart was into bootlegging?"

"Looks that way."

Virgil shook his head. "Why? His father-in-law is worth a million."

"Yeah, but that don't mean Bart gets any of it."

"Go to Wayne's and get his truck. We're going to confiscate all this."

"That's a lot of booze. How are we going to prove it belongs to Bart?"

"It's on his property." Virgil studied their surroundings. "However, it would be best if we caught him in the act of trying to unload his merchandise."

John grinned. "And, since he's been fired, he's probably in a hurry to unload all that before his daddy-in-law finds out what he's done."

Virgil tightened his jaw. "We're going to put that bastard where he belongs."

"But we still don't know who broke into Miss Cora's house."

"What if all that was just something to keep us busy tonight? Thinking one of us will park outside her house while the other sleeps."

John's face brightened. "We're going to be right here." He pointed across the alley at the empty warehouse that used to belong to the school district. "Right over there."

"Yeah, but let's leave the vehicle in front of Cora's house so Bart thinks it's safe to move."

"It's been a while since we've been on a stakeout."

"John, if Bart transports this hooch across a state line that would make it federal."

"You're right." John snapped his fingers. "We can get Hoover's guy, Gene McKinnon, from Joplin, to help us out."

"I'm driving back to the office. I'll call him and then drop the squad car off at Cora's like we planned. Let's just hope Gene gets here before Bart moves his merchandise."

"Make it snappy. I'll stand guard."

Virgil ran to the vehicle and took off for the station. He rolled up in front of the adjacent fire station and jumped out. Frank greeted him from the open bay. "Where's the fire?"

Glancing around, Virgil motioned for him to come to his office. Once inside, he picked up the office phone and dialed the FBI. Federal agent Gene McKinnon answered the phone on the other end.

"Gene, this is Virgil Carter in Parker County. We've targeted a bootlegger. He's got a shack full of bathtub whiskey. There are no federal seals on it."

"That's interesting."

"I think he's going to be moving it soon."

"Soon, like tonight?"

"Probably any minute."

"Okay, I'll head your way. I won't be there until after dark."

"My deputy and I will watch the place until you get here." Virgil gave him directions.

"I'm on my way."

Virgil turned to Frank, who wore a puzzled looked. "What's going on?"

"It all started when Cora and I came back from Joplin after a day of shopping. We got to her place and the door was open."

"She was robbed?"

Virgil didn't want to mention the underwear. "Nothing big, but when John and I went searching the neighborhood we ended up on Main Street. When we drove by the dry cleaners, I noticed the shed behind the store. Checked it out and found it loaded with bootleg whiskey from floor to ceiling."

Frank's mouth opened in surprise. "No kidding?"

"I wish I was. I left John there to keep an eye on things while I called the FBI."

"The Feds in on this?"

"Yes, it's their jurisdiction."

"What do you need from me?"

"I'm parking my squad car in front of Miss Williams' house then I'm going to join John." He went to the gun cabinet and took down the shotgun and a box of shells. "I may need your help if this goes south."

Frank took the shotgun. "I'm in."

Together they got back in the car and Virgil drove to Cora's. The house was quiet with the boys keeping a close eye on Pal.

"What's wrong?" Cora asked. "Did you find who broke in?"

"I'm not sure. It's beginning to look like a lot more than a simple break in. I'm leaving my car out front so whoever is behind this thinks I'm in the house with you."

Her hand flew to her mouth. "Oh, please be careful." She looked around. "Are we in danger?"

"Not if I can help it. Stay inside and lock the doors."

He and Frank left and headed for the dry cleaners. They saw John and decided that all three had to find a place where they couldn't be seen.

After several hours with nothing happening, Virgil thought perhaps Bart was going to wait until another time to move his stash.

Soon, FBI Agent Gene McKinnon pulled up in his unmarked car and parked between the two buildings where the vehicle couldn't be seen. As he approached, Virgil stepped out to shake hands. Gene and Virgil had known each other through a case they worked a few months back.

Two bums had decided to rob the Bank of Gibbs City and Virgil called in the FBI. Gene responded and they found the men responsible for the robbery along with the money.

Gene was married and had three boys. He was tall and lean as a whip. He smoked too much and coughed up a storm but he was a good lawman.

The agent pointed to the shed. "The booze in there?"

"Yeah, we didn't stop to count it but the damn thing is full all the way to the ceiling. No room to even enter the building."

Gene took off his Stetson and smoothed back his hair. "You think it's Bart Cooper?"

"That's my guess, since this is the building he worked at. His daddy-in-law owns the place, but Bart has been running the dry cleaners for several years."

Putting his hat back on, Gene said, "Okay, let's settle back and see who shows up."

"There's a loading dock over here. We're staked out behind the barrels." Virgil led the way. "Have you met my deputy, John?"

"Can't say I have." They shook hands. "Pleased to meet you."

Virgil put his hand on Frank's shoulder. "This is our Fire Chief, Frank Price."

Gene took out a smoke. "You guys want to take turns watching the place?"

"If he plans to move that stuff it has to be this weekend."

"Why?"

"Mr. Bridges fired him Friday. My guess is he wants this stuff out of here before someone gets too nosey. Plus, I figure he needs the money."

"You could be right. There's a beer joint over the Kansas line that's known to buy bootleg liquor. We've been keeping an eye on the place for a few months, but turned up cold."

John stepped back. "I hear something."

The sun had set and darkness crept closer. Wayne Jackson's truck came into view. Gears grinding, he backed it up to the door and killed the engine.

Two guys jumped out with the driver and they began loading the bed of the truck. Bart wasn't anywhere to be seen. John remained in the shadows. "Let's wait for a few minutes and see what happens."

It took over an hour for them to finally close the door and take off toward the south. "You think they're going to Kansas?"

"Don't know," Gene replied.

Virgil put his hand on Frank's shoulder. "I need you to keep an eye on the town should anything happen."

With a nod of agreement, Frank turned. "I'll head back to the office now."

They got into Gene's car and left with the headlights off. Virgil in the front seat, John sat in the back while the FBI agent drove.

After several miles, the truck turned off onto a dark, gravel road that Virgil recognized as leading to an abandoned farmhouse. Gene drove past the truck so they wouldn't suspect being followed. Up ahead, they pulled into a driveway and waited and watched. Soon another truck drove up with a vehicle behind following.

Four men moved the cases of liquor from Wayne's truck to another that Virgil had never seen. Bart Cooper stood to the side directing all the action.

"They're over the state line," Virgil said. "Let's move in."

Gene flipped on his headlight and the siren, two men took off running into the field, but John went after them. Virgil held his gun on Bart.

"What you boys doing?" Gene asked.

"Nothing that's any of your business."

Gene pulled out his gun. "If that's hooch, it's my business." He flashed his FBI badge. "You're under arrest for transporting illegal alcohol across a state line."

"You can't prove this is mine. I'm just helping these guys out."

"Wrong, we discovered the liquor back in Gibbs City, on property you used to manage." Gene slapped the handcuffs on Bart.

Virgil chuckled. "I had a feeling you'd be behind bars before all this was said and done."

CHAPTER THREE

Cora tossed and turned, unable to fall asleep. Mr. Clevenger had stubbornly refused to leave her and Jack alone. So, he lay snoring on her couch while she kept checking on Pal.

Sometime in the early morning, she woke to the aroma of coffee. She quickly dressed, washed her face, brushed her teeth and hair then moved to the kitchen.

Mr. Clevenger sat at the kitchen table petting Pal, who rested comfortably on his lap.

She approached. "How's he doing?"

"He's a tough rascal. He went to the bathroom and I didn't see any blood."

She let out a tired breath. "That's good."

"He managed to drink a little milk out of a saucer, but then he just fell back to sleep."

She rubbed the dog's head. "Poor thing is probably exhausted."

"Don't imagine he feels too good either."

"My guess is, whoever came in the house kicked him."

"That or hit him with something." The dog yawned and lowered his head. "Pal here wasn't about to let some hoodlum come into his house."

She straightened. "I'm so glad he was here, but I hate that he was hurt."

"Aw, animals are tougher than we give them credit for. And this one's a scrapper."

She poured them coffee and slumped in the chair while Mr. Clevenger put the dog back in the room with the boys. When he returned, he took a sip of his coffee and smiled. "I'm just glad you and little Jack are okay."

Not wanting to seem ungrateful, Cora put her hand on the old man's and squeezed. "I appreciate you staying here last night."

Mr. Clevenger moved his hand, apparently uncomfortable with the show of affection. "I only stayed because I wanted to shoot the idiot with my shotgun. I'd have filled him full of buckshot."

She smiled. "I'm glad it didn't come to that." She noticed he'd placed his weapon on the counter. "I felt protected."

She hadn't felt that way in a very long time. Usually the opposite, but she knew her neighbor was willing to defend her home against anyone who came against her.

The feeling touched her heart.

"How about some breakfast?"

Mr. Clevenger stiffened. "Whatcha got in mind?"

"How about some bacon and eggs and gravy?"

A doubtful scowled covered his face. "You fixin' to tell me you know how to make gravy?"

She smiled. "I am."

"Well, I'll be the judge of that."

Finishing her coffee, Cora put on a pan of biscuits and refilled Mr. Clevenger's cup. While the bread baked she asked, "Did you know there are several fruit trees in the backyard?"

"I know they're there, but they ain't never been taken care of."

"Why did Aunt Rose plant them in if she wasn't going to try to get fruit?"

"She didn't. Thomas did."

"JJ's father?"

Mr. Clevenger nodded. "Now there was a man who could grow anything. He put in the best garden in town right there in Rose's backyard."

"Really?" She remembered picking vegetables from the garden, but she'd never seen any fruit. "I'm glad he was so helpful to Aunt Rose."

"The only things Rose could grow were weeds and roses. If she planted a rose, the next thing you knew, she had a whole field of 'em."

"That's lovely."

"Weren't to me. Damn thorns tore up my hands."

"You have to be careful cutting roses."

"She got my Wanda into growing some, she did."

"They were friends?"

"She and my Wanda grew up together. That's the reason we bought the house next door. They wanted to be close. Like sisters."

"Then how come you and Aunt Rose didn't get along?"

He batted his hand. "Aw, we got along okay. We used to do more fussing than anything else."

"She called you Satan."

He chuckled. "Well, I called her worse than that."

When the biscuits were almost done, Cora sliced several slabs of bacon and put them in the cast iron skillet. Soon the aroma filled the house.

Virgil called from the back door. "You up already?"

Mr. Clevenger turned to the sound. "Howdy, sheriff."

Virgil came in and she handed him a cup of coffee. "Did you find anything?"

Virgil pulled out a chair and sat across from Mr. Clevenger. "We found Bart was bootlegging."

Mr. Clevenger leaned closer. "You don't say."

"That shed in the back of the dry cleaners was piled full of whiskey."

Cora wrinkled her forehead. "I often wondered what was in there. I assumed it was chemicals used in the cleaning machine."

"No, it was liquor."

Mr. Clevenger took a sip of coffee. "Did he confess to breaking into missy's house?"

"Not exactly. A guy named Andy Bergman was with Bart and he had torn trousers and a pretty good bite on his leg."

Mr. Clevenger shook his head. "Never heard of him."

"He's not from around here. He lives over in Farmersville."

"Why would he rob my house?"

"I think it's something Bart put him up to so I'd be here protecting you instead of investigating him moving his moonshine operation."

Mr. Clevenger stood and brought the coffeepot back to the table and filled cups. "Damn, I didn't know Bart had such a diabolical mind."

Virgil took a sip of coffee. "I'm just glad Cora wasn't here alone."

She took out the egg carton. "Me too." She looked at Mr. Clevenger. "How do you want your eggs cooked?"

Virgil glanced at the stove. "You fixing breakfast?"

She smiled. "Mr. Clevenger stayed here all night to protect us. Kept his shotgun right by his side."

Her neighbor beamed. "Over easy, with the whites done." He pointed at Cora. "I'm mighty fussy about my eggs."

She winked at Virgil. "I'll do my best."

Virgil glanced at her. "I'll take mine any way you want to cook them."

"Of course, you will," Mr. Clevenger huffed. "You're just looking for a handout."

Virgil laughed. "I was up all night running down criminals."

"Humph, lollygagging is all you're doing."

Cora enjoyed the two men's comfortable banter and the look of sheer delight as she placed Mr. Clevenger's plate in front of him. "I hope these are good enough."

She cooked Virgil's eggs and watched as her neighbor bit into his perfectly fried eggs, biscuits covered with gravy and crispy fried bacon.

"That looks mighty good, Earl."

Mr. Clevenger chuckled. "It does, but you wait your turn."

Cora placed Virgil's plate down before frying her own breakfast. They ate in silence, except for Mr. Clevenger moaning softly every time he sunk his teeth into a bite of biscuits and gravy.

Virgil wiped his mouth. "Best food I've ever eaten, Cora."

"Thank you." She glanced at her neighbor. "How about you, Mr. Clevenger?"

"Call me Earl." He chewed slowly. "Not bad. Not bad at all."

"Of course, I know it's not as good as Wanda's."

"Nope, nope it ain't. Cause she was the best cook in the county."

Virgil shoved the last bit in his mouth. "I'm not so sure about that. Cora beats anyone's I ever tasted."

"That's because you never tasted anything Wanda cooked."

"I think I did. When I was a young boy she used to cook for the church socials. She was good, but Cora's better."

"Now there you go spouting off about stuff you don't know nothing about. 'Sides, you only say that because you're sweet on missy here."

Virgil reddened a little and Cora stood to clear the table. "You both stop fussing. You'll wake up the boys."

"You can say whatever you want, Earl. But Cora is the best cook I know."

"That's 'cause you don't know any." Earl stood, took his shotgun and walked out the back door.

Cora stepped to the back door and called, "Thank you for looking after us."

Earl turned back, saluted, and walked toward his home. "You're welcome."

Cora popped Virgil with the dish towel. "You two argue too much."

Virgil laughed and filled both their cups. "That's because his wife wasn't that good at much of anything except being completely devoted to him."

"Well, they were happy together."

Virgil smiled. "That they were. Still walking around holding hands just days before she died."

"What about their children. Do they live close by?"

Virgil ran his finger around the rim of his cup. "I don't know what happened, but Wanda never could have children. She lost every child she conceived."

Cora's heart sank and she lowered her gaze. "Oh, that's so sad."

"Yes, it was. My mother always felt so sorry for her. Then she went into the hospital and my mother mentioned that she'd never have another miscarriage again."

"That's too bad." She glanced out the back door. "I know he's so lonely. Living over there with no family."

"His father was killed in the Great War then a year later he lost his older brother in Britain."

"So many lost so much during the war."

Virgil stood and went to the sink. "It left a lot of scars behind and some people still haven't mended yet."

"Do you ever think about the war, Virgil?"

"All the time. But I try to stay in the here and now. If a man keeps fighting in his head, he's no use to anyone."

"Is that Carl's problem?"

"I don't know. I'd like to think as time goes on he'll get better, but I'm not so sure."

"We all have wounds."

He looked at her, his blue eyes intense and deep. "You've had your share of bad memories too, Cora."

"Yes, but mine were of my own making."

"What happened?"

Jack stuck his head around the corner. "Aunt Cora, is Pal okay?"

She smiled, hugging Jack against her chest. "I think he's going to be okay. He'll have to heal, but I bet he's back to normal in no time."

She watched as Jack went into the living room and ran a gentle hand over Pal. "He's a good dog."

Virgil bent down to rub the dog's fur. "He's a brave little dog. If he hadn't been here, we don't know what would've happened."

"Did you catch the bad guys?"

"I don't know yet, I'm getting ready to drive to Joplin and find out."

CHAPTER FOUR

Virgil got in his squad car and headed out of town. He wanted to question Bart to see if he had anything to do with the break in at Cora's house. If Bergman did the deed, Bart put him up to it because Andy didn't appear that smart.

He arrived at the FBI office in Joplin and went looking for Gene. They ran into each other in the hallway. "You get anything out of them?"

"They're all pretty quiet for now. Cooper is screaming for a lawyer, but he's going to wait. I have men counting the bottles and a revenuer trying to figure out what still Cooper used to get the whiskey. We don't think he's running anything as labor intensive as a still by himself."

"You're probably right there. Bart spent most days at the cleaners. He's always had a little sweet piece on the side, if you know what I mean. The last one I sent home with her face pretty messed up."

"That's a shame." They walked toward the interrogating room. "I figure the two with him are just helpers. They aren't smart enough for much else. I've pegged Cooper for the leader of the operation."

"Any idea who the buyer is?"

"Yeah, a fella named Paul White. He buys cheap whiskey then pours it into his used bottles with tax stickers on them. This way it's hard to prove he's selling moonshine."

They walked into the room where Bart sat cuffed to the table. "You better get me out of here," he screamed.

Bart's appearance surprised Virgil. Not that he was a dandy dresser or anything, but he'd never seen the man dirty his hands. How he sat in the bare room, his hair sticking up, clothes drenched in sweat and the smell of rot gut whiskey clinging to his body.

Gene pulled up a chair. "You're not going anywhere."

"I didn't break the law and you can't prove I have."

"What are you doing with a truckload of illegal booze?"

"That's not my liquor. I was just hitching a ride to my brother's in Kansas."

"I hope your friends are singing the same tune."

"They're all liars and you can't prove a damn thing on me." Bart puffed out his chest. "Just try."

"Oh, we'll prove something. You being out on a back road in the middle of the night in a truck loaded down with hooch is enough alone."

"Not if I'm just hitchhiking."

"We'll talk to the others and see what they say." Virgil turned to Bart. "Did you have that Bergman boy break into Cora's house?"

"You trying to blame me for a house break in, too?"

"Just asking."

"I don't know nothin' about her house getting broken into or anything else."

Virgil scratched his head. "Well, I'll have to do some more investigating because someone broke in and stole a diamond broach her grandmother gave her. It's worth a small fortune."

Bart's eyes widened and he leaned forward. "What'd you say?"

"I said, whoever broke into her house got away with something valuable."

"She ain't got nothing worth stealing. If she did she wouldn't have been begging me for a job."

"It's a family heirloom or something. She's been saving it for an emergency."

Bart's gaze traveled around the room. His brushy brows low and squeezed tight together. "She's lying."

"No, I saw it once. Nice looking piece of jewelry. Probably worth more than all that whiskey you got caught with."

Bart's jaw tightened. "I don't believe a damn word you're saying."

"I think you're wondering if little Andy pocketed something of value that he's not sharing."

Bart turned aside. "I don't know what you're talking about."

"We'll see."

Gene touched Virgil on the arm. "Let's go next door."

"You tell that son of a bitch he opens his mouth, I'll gut him."

Gene looked at Bart. "We'll be sure and relay that message to your friend."

As they left, Bart screamed. "You're going to pay for this…"

They walked into the room with Andy Bergman, who looked scared to death. He couldn't' be any more than twenty years old. Bad way to start a man's life.

Virgil pulled out a chair across from the young man. "You ready to talk?"

"I ain't saying a damn thing."

"Okay, we'll be sending a man in for you soon. A federal judge will decide what to do with you."

One on each arm, Gene and Virgil took Andy to the room occupied by Bart. After leaving the two criminals alone, Virgil and Gene stood outside the door, listening.

"Where is that broach, you cheater?"

"What broach?"

"Shhh, keep your voice down. Virgil told me you got away with a piece of jewelry worth a fortune."

"Yeah, a fella named Paul White. He buys cheap whiskey then pours it into his used bottles with tax stickers on them. This way it's hard to prove he's selling moonshine."

They walked into the room where Bart sat cuffed to the table. "You better get me out of here," he screamed.

Bart's appearance surprised Virgil. Not that he was a dandy dresser or anything, but he'd never seen the man dirty his hands. How he sat in the bare room, his hair sticking up, clothes drenched in sweat and the smell of rot gut whiskey clinging to his body.

Gene pulled up a chair. "You're not going anywhere."

"I didn't break the law and you can't prove I have."

"What are you doing with a truckload of illegal booze?"

"That's not my liquor. I was just hitching a ride to my brother's in Kansas."

"I hope your friends are singing the same tune."

"They're all liars and you can't prove a damn thing on me." Bart puffed out his chest. "Just try."

"Oh, we'll prove something. You being out on a back road in the middle of the night in a truck loaded down with hooch is enough alone."

"Not if I'm just hitchhiking."

"We'll talk to the others and see what they say." Virgil turned to Bart. "Did you have that Bergman boy break into Cora's house?"

"You trying to blame me for a house break in, too?"

"Just asking."

"I don't know nothin' about her house getting broken into or anything else."

Virgil scratched his head. "Well, I'll have to do some more investigating because someone broke in and stole a diamond broach her grandmother gave her. It's worth a small fortune."

Bart's eyes widened and he leaned forward. "What'd you say?"

"I said, whoever broke into her house got away with something valuable."

"She ain't got nothing worth stealing. If she did she wouldn't have been begging me for a job."

"It's a family heirloom or something. She's been saving it for an emergency."

Bart's gaze traveled around the room. His brushy brows low and squeezed tight together. "She's lying."

"No, I saw it once. Nice looking piece of jewelry. Probably worth more than all that whiskey you got caught with."

Bart's jaw tightened. "I don't believe a damn word you're saying."

"I think you're wondering if little Andy pocketed something of value that he's not sharing."

Bart turned aside. "I don't know what you're talking about."

"We'll see."

Gene touched Virgil on the arm. "Let's go next door."

"You tell that son of a bitch he opens his mouth, I'll gut him."

Gene looked at Bart. "We'll be sure and relay that message to your friend."

As they left, Bart screamed. "You're going to pay for this..."

They walked into the room with Andy Bergman, who looked scared to death. He couldn't' be any more than twenty years old. Bad way to start a man's life.

Virgil pulled out a chair across from the young man. "You ready to talk?"

"I ain't saying a damn thing."

"Okay, we'll be sending a man in for you soon. A federal judge will decide what to do with you."

One on each arm, Gene and Virgil took Andy to the room occupied by Bart. After leaving the two criminals alone, Virgil and Gene stood outside the door, listening.

"Where is that broach, you cheater?"

"What broach?"

"Shhh, keep your voice down. Virgil told me you got away with a piece of jewelry worth a fortune."

"All I got away with was my leg practically being torn off by that damn dog. I couldn't shake the rat. They had to take me to see the doctor. I'll probably catch rabies."

"I'll kill you if you don't tell me. Don't you be holding out on me!"

Virgil looked at Gene. "You heard enough?"

"Yeah, let's do the paperwork and get these guys locked up."

Virgil felt good driving back to Gibbs City. He remembered his and Cora's trip Saturday and how much fun they'd had just being together. That was the best day he'd experienced since returning home from the war. He like being around her and Jack was like the son he'd always wanted.

But her past lay between them like a thick curtain. He didn't know what had led up to her going to prison and no one else wanted to discuss the situation. He was tempted to go to her father and learn the truth, but he had no right.

Besides, her father could be the very reason Cora ended up in jail. Also, just because she had custody of Jack didn't mean his real father wouldn't someday come looking for him.

Cora loved Jack. If there was ever a threat to him, she'd be like a momma bear protecting her cub. He had made a copy of those papers she gave him. Maybe it was time he looked into her past a little closer.

He wished she'd trust him enough to talk about the situation, but she refused and he wouldn't judge her on that account because he didn't know what she'd been through. He could guess, but he had no proof.

At the fire station, he told Frank what happened and took a warm bath then went to his tiny room to rest. Sitting on the side of the narrow bed, he realized he was beginning to hate the little cubbyhole.

It saddened him to think of Cora's warm and inviting home with Jack always glad to see him. He couldn't help but wonder if something like that could ever be his.

Was he meant to be alone and empty? Usually on Saturday night, he went to Mable's for a little recreation, but that didn't appeal to him when he thought of Cora. She certainly wouldn't approve.

After a nap, he freshened up and went to Betty's Diner for something to eat. He ran into several citizens who were curious as to why the FBI was investigating the dry cleaners. Things didn't happen in a small town that someone didn't know something about, and was eager to share the gossip.

Virgil had John explain to Mr. Bridges what had happened so there'd be no surprise coming at him. Needless to say, Arthur wasn't going to be too happy with Bart and probably hoped Virgil threw the book at him.

On the way back to the station, he saw Cora out in the front yard with little Ronnie, a towel wrapped around his skinny shoulders. Virgil stopped and got out of the vehicle.

"What's going on?"

"Ronnie is getting a haircut and not happy about it."

Ronnie had his face scrunched up like he had a mouth full of pickles.

Virgil leaned down. "This is the cleanest I've seen you in a long time, young man."

"Miss Cora made me take a bath."

"Well, I'd say that's a big improvement."

"I don't think so."

Cora stepped forward and touched the little boy's shoulder. "You made a deal, Ronnie."

"What kind of deal?"

"I told her if she'd fix them chocolate chip pancakes Jack's been talking about, I'd take a bath."

"And did she?"

Ronnie smiled. "Yeah, and they were really good."

Virgil knelt in front of Ronnie. "So, what's your beef?"

"I never agreed to a haircut."

"Ronnie your hair is too long and shaggy. I'm just going to trim it up a little. It won't hurt a bit. Now wait here while I get the clippers."

Virgil watched as Cora went into the house. She looked so pretty today. Always clean and well-dressed, she made his heart do all kinds of crazy stuff. "Sheriff, will you cut my hair instead of her?"

Virgil straightened. "Why don't you want Miss Cora to cut your hair?"

"Cause she's a girl."

"She's an adult and she's probably better at cutting hair than I am."

"But, she's still a girl. I don't want a girl to cut my hair."

Virgil wished it wasn't Sunday. He'd take Ronnie down to the barbershop and let Leonard give him a haircut, but she seemed determined to do it today.

Cora came out of the house and Virgil stepped on the porch to greet her. "He wants me to cut his hair."

She looked surprised. "Why?"

"You're a girl."

"That's no reason. He's just trying to worm his way out of getting his hair cut."

Virgil shrugged. "I agree. And you'd probably do a better job than I can, but Ronnie hasn't had a lot of contact with females in his life. It probably feels awkward to him."

She reluctantly turned over the scissors, clippers, and comb to Virgil, who approached the young boy. "You're probably going to regret this."

Ronnie shrugged. "It's just hair. It'll grow back."

Cora leaned forward. "Why didn't you think like that when I wanted to cut your hair?"

"You're a girl. And girls shouldn't cut men's hair."

"Who on earth told you that?"

"My daddy."

Cora crossed her arms tightly and pressed her lips together. She glared at Virgil like he and Ronnie were in on the conspiracy together.

"Okay, hold still." Virgil put his hand on Ronnie's head and tilted it to the left and clipped around his ear. He backed up and eyed his job. Satisfied with his progress so far, he continued. When he finished the other ear he winced. That side didn't look quite the same. The hair was much higher on the right side than the left.

He made a minor adjustment and continued. Brown hair covered the sidewalk and Ronnie kept wiggling until Virgil was about to lose his patience. "You have to hold still."

"I'm trying, but it itches."

"I'm almost done."

Using the clippers he went around the base of his head and evened everything up. "Close your eyes while I cut the front." That's when Virgil ran into trouble. No matter how many times he tried, he couldn't cut a straight line so he kept trying to compensate.

Cora stood watching. An air of superiority had her tapping her toe. "You should stop now before he's completely bald."

Ronnie cried out, "I don't wanna be bald."

Virgil stood back and cringed. "That's not too bad."

"It looks like you cut his hair with the push mower."

"I agree it needs a little…" Virgil moved his hand back and forth. "A little touch up here and there."

"It looks horrible."

"I'll take him to the barbershop tomorrow."

"He has school tomorrow."

"Well, after he gets home."

"The kids will make fun of him."

"No, they won't." He tried to make light of the situation with a little humor. "Boys get crazy haircuts all the time. I had a few myself."

"And how was it showing up at school?"

Terrible.

He remembered it had been humiliating and the kids laughed at him. Of course, he beat up most of them, but little Ronnie wasn't big enough to defend a horrible haircut.

"Ronnie get in the car." He looked at Cora. "I'll see if I can get Leonard to open his shop."

"Good luck." With her nose in the air, she took the instruments from his hands and walked back into the house.

Virgil wanted to remind her that this wasn't his idea but he knew it wouldn't do any good.

With Ronnie sitting next to him, Virgil started the car and drove to the barbershop. Leonard and his wife lived upstairs. Going around to the back of the building, they climbed the stairs and knocked on the door.

After a few minutes, Patricia Casey, Leonard's wife answered the door with a dour expression covering her aging face. "What do you want, Sheriff?"

"Is Leonard here?"

The barber appeared behind his wife. "What you need?"

"Can you open your shop?"

"I don't work on Sundays. That's the Lord's day."

Virgil reached behind him and took Ronnie by the arm and placed the boy in front of him. "This is an emergency."

"Good God Almighty, what did you do to that boy's hair?"

Ronnie grinned. Of course, he hadn't been near a mirror. "The sheriff gave me a haircut."

Virgil wanted to hide. "I've never done that before and this is why."

Leonard rubbed his long chin, and stared down at the little boy. "It'll cost you double."

"I don't care. Just fix it."

They followed Leonard down the stairs and waited for him to unlock his shop door. Once inside, Leonard flipped the lock and motioned for Ronnie to climb onto the chair after he'd placed a board over the arms so Ronnie sat higher.

Ronnie got the first glance of his haircut. "Golly, Sheriff. That looks really bad."

"I know, son, and I'm sorry. I think you should've went with Miss Cora."

Ronnie leaned closer, turning his head from side to side. "I think you might be right."

Leonard put the cape around Ronnie's neck and went to work. Virgil promised himself that day, he'd never try to cut hair again. In a matter of minutes he realized if he'd been expecting a miracle from Leonard, it wasn't coming.

When the cape was removed and Leonard brushed the loose hair from Ronnie's back, Virgil didn't see a lot of improvement.

"Mr. Casey," Ronnie said. "I don't think you cut hair much better than the sheriff."

"You listen here, you little ungrateful brat. I didn't have a lot to work with."

"But now it's sticking straight up like a porcupine."

"That's because right here on your crown the hair isn't even an inch long. That you can thank the sheriff for."

Virgil put Ronnie in the car and dreaded facing Cora. "We really made a mess of things, Ronnie."

"I didn't do nothing."

"Well, you should've let Miss Cora cut your hair."

"Yeah, but I didn't know you was gonna scalp me."

"I told you I didn't know what I was doing."

"I just figured you had to be better than a woman."

"Well, sometimes a woman can do things better than a man." He turned the corner. "You think I can make those chocolate chip pancakes as good as Miss Cora?"

"No, and I don't want you to try. You'd just ruin 'em."

"See, same thing with haircuts. She's probably better at that than me."

"I think Jack could do a better job than you."

"Then ask him next time."

Ronnie ran his hand over the top of his hair. "It feels kinda funny. And my head's lighter."

"It's different, but honestly Ronnie, it's better than it was."

"I kind of like it. No other kid has a haircut like this. And it was the first time I ever sat in the barber chair. That was fun."

"Let's just hope Miss Cora is okay with it. I think we might've hurt her feelings."

They arrived at the house and Jack came bouncing down the stairs. "Did you get your hair cut, Ronnie?"

When Ronnie got out of the car, Jack blinked several times. "Hey, you look different. I want my hair like that."

Ronnie rubbed his head. "And look, you can't mess it up."

"Yeah, lucky you, you don't even have to comb your hair."

"And if it was summer, it'd be really cool."

"But now that winter is coming on, you'd better wear a hat."

Cora stepped out on the porch and stopped. "That's a burr."

"That's the best Leonard could do. And the old grouch charged me double."

"I like it, Miss Cora, don't you?"

"Well, it's kind of different."

"Look, I don't have to ever comb my hair again."

She frowned at Virgil, who could only lean against the car, cross his ankle and swallow the insult.

While the boys rushed over to show Tommy, she put her hands on her hips and cracked a smile. "Remind me to never let you cut hair again."

"Oh, you don't have to worry about that."

"Would you like to join us for a picnic?"

His heart skipped a beat and his chest tightened. "That would be nice."

"Come in and you can carry the basket."

"How's Pal?"

"He's much better. He's going with us."

Virgil headed across the street. "I'll get the boys."

He returned with Tommy, Ronnie and Jack in tow. Everyone grabbed something to carry for the picnic. In a couple of blocks they sat at the park, under the same tree Virgil had seen her and Jack at before, and spread out their blanket.

They'd put the food out and Virgil looked up to see Ronnie's dad, Warren stalking their way. His fists balled, his head lowered, Virgil knew this wasn't going to be pretty.

CHAPTER FIVE

Cora sat on the blanket removing the plates from the basket when Virgil stood, his stance hard, his glare determined. She looked behind her to see Warren stomping toward them. She jumped to her feet, immediately putting Ronnie behind her.

"Where's my boy?"

Cora could tell he was already half-drunk. "He's right here. We're getting ready to have a picnic."

"No, he ain't. He's coming home."

"Pa, can't I play here?"

Warren pointed his finger at the little boy. "You shut up or I'll knock your teeth out."

Virgil moved closer to her and Ronnie. "There's no need to threaten the kid."

Then Ronnie came out and Warren narrowed his eye. "What the hell happened to your hair?"

"I got a haircut."

Warren stepped closer to Cora, his eyes red with anger. "You think you got the right to do anything you want to my son. He belongs to me and you ain't got the right."

"I simply gave him a bath last night and my intent was to trim his hair a little. The ordeal wasn't successful so he went to the barber."

"Who told you that would be okay?"

"I did it." Virgil said. "You got something to say, say it to me."

Warren shook his fist at the sheriff. "I'll tell you what. I'm going to the damn judge and report you. Ain't right that you stick your nose where it don't belong."

Cora spoke up. "We were only helping Ronnie."

"He don't need your help."

Virgil stepped between Warren and Cora. "He needs someone's help because you're nothing but a lazy, good for nothing drunk."

"Ronnie, you get home right now."

Warren started taking off his belt and Ronnie ran for home screaming. "Please don't whip me, pa. Please don't whip me."

Cora stood next to Virgil and glared.

Virgil said, "You touch that child and I'll turn you in to the state."

"You can't do nothing."

He stepped closer and Virgil shoved him back. "Don't push your luck, Warren. And I'd be pleased if you talked to Judge Garner. I'm sure he'd hear from Miss Potter and the neighbors exactly how you treat your son."

Warren turned and walked away.

"I hope Ronnie doesn't get into trouble."

"Legally all we can do is standby and hope the kid doesn't get hurt too badly."

"I don't understand. If he doesn't care about Ronnie, why does it bother him that someone else does?"

"He's a bitter man. Been that way all his life."

"What happened to Ronnie's mother?"

"She died when Ronnie was born. Doc said she bled to death. For a while Warren's mother took the child. When he was about three, she had a stroke and passed away. That's when Ronnie came to live with his dad."

"Is that when he started drinking?"

"No, he's been a drunk since I've known him."

"How long is that?"

"Since he was a teenager. His daddy was a pretty decent man but he was killed in the mines when Warren was about ten. His mother raised him by herself."

Jack ran up. "Where's Ronnie?"

"He had to go home."

"Oh, I thought he'd get to be in our picnic."

"No, his father needed him."

Tommy and Jack ate quickly then ran to play. Cora saw that Virgil had lost his appetite. And so had she. God only knew what Ronnie was going through. Somehow she had to protect that little boy. No matter what, Warren couldn't be allowed to continue abusing the boy.

Soon they decided to call it a day because Cora had to work tomorrow and the boys had school. Virgil helped them carry everything back to the house and helped her clean up while Jack listened to his radio show then got ready for bed.

"Would you like a cup of coffee before you go home?"

"Thanks, that sounds like a great idea."

She put the coffee on then went to supervise Jack's bedtime routine. After tucking him in, she joined Virgil at the table and they enjoyed a cup of coffee.

"Are you hungry?" she asked.

"No, Warren did a good job of killing my appetite."

"I noticed that. I'm sorry, but there isn't much we can do about it."

"I could call the county child place, but they'd take him and put him in a reform school or an orphanage. Boys come out of there worse than when they go in. Ronnie's so young."

"Can't someone adopt him?"

"Not unless Warren is willing to give him up and that would be tough. Not only is he miserable, he wants to make his son's life a living hell, too."

"There should be a law."

"There should be a lot of laws."

"I'm glad you at least have Bart locked up. That makes me feel safer."

"I'm glad Jack fought for Pal. He's proved to be quite the protector."

Cora smiled. "He really has. I hope he continues to improve."

"He was moving around at the park pretty good."

"I noticed that. Jack would be broken-hearted if anything happened to the dog. That's why I worry about him running loose. What if he were hit by a car?"

"Pal stays pretty close to the house. He knows where his food is."

"I've meant to thank you all weekend for taking us to Joplin. I'm glad we got the things I need."

"Starting next week, I'll get to work on those projects in the evenings."

"Maybe I can pay JJ."

"JJ has a family. I don't have anyone waiting for me when I get off work."

She looked at him and tilted her head. "I don't even know where you live."

"I stay at the station. There's a small room. I bunk in there. No need for a home, I'm never there."

"So, the sheriff must be single?"

"No, if I had a family I'd get a house, but just for me I don't see the need. Besides, who'd clean it?"

She laughed. "Oh, so it's because you're lazy."

"I guess you could say that." He stood and put on his hat. "Well, I'd better go. You have a job to go to tomorrow."

"I'm excited."

"Helen spoke up for you. That means a lot around here."

"I'm grateful she did. I certainly need the job. I wasn't looking forward to job hunting."

Cora thought for a moment. "What's going to happen to Bart?"

"Since his crime was federal, he won't be getting out anytime soon."

"It's not nice to say, but I'm glad. He was such a creep."

"I've never figured out what Ester saw in him."

"Haven't you heard, love is blind?"

He smiled and her heart fluttered in her chest. "I think I might have heard that."

At the door, she watched him drive away. Her heart ached for him. He had to be lonely without anyone in his life.

At least she had Jack and that was a blessing. He was the single most wonderful thing that'd happened to her. He was her future and everything she did was for him.

Pal scratched at the door signaling he needed to relieve himself before she prepared for bed. The tough little guy moved around better by the minute. He made sure everything was out of his yard before finally coming in for the night.

No direction needed. Pal rushed in the door and did his duty, took a drink of water then trotted into Jack room where he curled up on the rug in front of the bed.

Humming softly, she cleaned and prepared the coffeepot for tomorrow morning. She'd just turned off the living room light when a pounding at the back door had Pal shooting out of the bedroom, barking loudly.

Who would be calling at such a late hour? Looking down she noticed the hair on Pal's back stood up. She cracked the door a little and saw Warren standing on the steps. Opening a little wider, she asked, "Yes?"

He shook his fist. "This is a warning for you and you better listen. That sheriff ain't gonna be able to protect you if you keep sticking your nose in my business. Ronnie ain't your kid. You understand? Or do I need to come in there and teach you a thing or two?"

Pal barked and scratched at the door wanting to get to Warren.

Earl walked into her yard, his shotgun aimed at Warren's back. "You better hightail it out of here or I'll fill your ass full of buckshot. Ya hear?"

Warren staggered then turned around. "You ain't gonna shoot nobody."

Earl cocked the shotgun and looked down the barrel. "You don't get across the street where you belong, we're about to find out."

Warren left, falling twice before Earl would lower his weapon. "That low down skunk. I ought to shoot him just to make sure my shotgun's still sighted."

"That man is a nuisance. And God only knows what poor Ronnie is going through."

"I know that's the truth. The man cares more for his hooch than his own kid."

"Thank you for coming to my rescue."

"Don't open the door when it's dark. You never can tell who's standing on the other side."

"From now on I'll follow your advice." She waved. "Good night, Earl."

She closed the door and leaned back, her heart pounding so hard she feared it would jump from her chest. She put her hand to her chest. What a monster.

She went to bed that night afraid Warren would come back to argue or maybe he'd burn down the house around them. No one knew what a drunk was capable of.

CHAPTER SIX

Virgil checked in with Frank then went into his office. He'd been tied up most of the weekend, so there were several things he needed to tend to before calling it a day.

John had left notes on a few disturbances he'd dealt with on Sunday then he went home.

Comfortable that Bart wouldn't be causing Cora any more trouble, Virgil got ready for bed. Exhausted from too little sleep, it didn't take long for him to fall into a deep slumber.

The night was freezing. Cold and foggy, damp and chilled to the bone. He sat hunkered down in a foxhole like the rest of his unit. His body trembled and his hands felt like blocks of ice.

He hadn't slept in days and there was no chow yesterday or today. The afternoon sun was somewhere behind the smoking frost that settled on his shoulders and icy chill that had him shivering.

Several of the men in his platoon were shouting back and forth to each other. That's how they stayed awake for long periods of time. And a way to find out who was still alive.

They'd expected reinforcements and supplies two days ago but nothing came. According to his forward man, there wasn't anything out there but Germans waiting for them to stick up their heads.

Occasionally shots rang out in the distance and a grenade went off, but mostly it was eerily quiet and scary as hell.

They hadn't been rushed because Virgil figured the Germans were in the same boat they were. Short on food, ammo, men and energy. But still, nobody wanted to give any ground to the enemy. Lives depended on them staying alert.

Virgil worried about a young soldier who'd joined the group a few days ago. He was fresh out of training and green as a summer apple. He was scared and lost in a strange country fighting a war he knew nothing about.

Virgil knew where he was and waited for him to call out. "Okay guys, time for roll call. Let's see who's awake."

Names came from every direction and every state. There were fifty-two men when he set out. Now he was down to twenty-one. All the others had been killed or captured. He knew two kilometers away a line of German tanks sat waiting for the command to move forward. He hoped help came from somewhere before that happened because twenty-one hungry, cold, inexperienced men couldn't hold off a whole army of Germans.

Satisfied when he heard the New Yorker's name, Virgil hunkered deeper into his coat. "Be sure to keep your helmets on. They could save your life."

He knew that was a hard request because they were steel and they became cold and held in very little body heat. He wished the damn fog would lift so they could make out what was going on around them. Earlier yesterday, the Germans had been able to walk right into their encampment and start shooting men in their foxholes.

They couldn't even bury the poor bastards because the damn ground was frozen solid. He couldn't remember a time when he'd been this cold. Freezing conditions often lured a man to sleep and he'd never wake up.

Virgil crawled out of his foxhole and made his rounds. Cheering as he went to make sure the men were okay. He listened to them bitch and complain knowing there wasn't a damn thing he could do but stand beside them and take the same punishment.

He came to Jamison and Hensley's foxhole and found the two huddled together trying to stay warm. "Keep your weapons nearby. A Kraut could walk up on you and kill you before you had a chance to move."

He visited several other foxholes until he came to those on the outer perimeter. They were the closest to the enemy. He looked down into the hiding places to find seven of the men had been bayonetted. He quickly looked around. Leaning over he felt the blood was still warm.

It'd just happened. At that time, a German came behind him and jumped on his back. Virgil flipped him over and stabbed him in the chest. He wondered how many more there were out there prowling for soldiers to kill.

"Men, keep your heads up, we have a bounty hunter in the midst. Stay alert."

He moved onward trying to find the line. He heard faint sounds and as he crawled in the freezing snow, the language was German. Those troops weren't twenty feet away from his men.

Scooting backwards, he made it to each man and ordered them to move back as quietly as possible. To head for a line of trees he remembered but couldn't see. As the men fell out, he kept his gun at the ready.

Tension pulled every muscle in his body, his hands hurt from the cold and he wasn't sure he could pull the trigger if he had to. He no longer felt his feet and he was so hungry his head spun like a top.

Determined to get his men to safety, he pushed them to get to the tree line.

Then the Germans opened fire from behind and the front of their line. Bullets zinged in every direction. Virgil fell to one knee and started firing. Grenades exploded and men screamed. The Krauts moved toward them, their guns firing so fast it was like watching a flamethrower.

He kept fighting. The young soldier fell next to him and tears filled his eyes. He thought of his men, of their families, and how unfair all this was.

"No, no, no!" Virgil jerked upright and sat in his bed trembling. He was freezing even though it wasn't that cold. Sweat soaked him and his bedding. He swung his feet over the side of the bed but didn't dare try to stand.

It would be several minutes before his heart would slow down, his hands would calm and his eyes cleared. He took a few deep breaths and clutched the side of the mattress. Willing his mind to forget. Reminding himself it was just a dream. That many of his men got out of that situation. He got out.

He'd come home, yet so many had died there in the frozen Ardennes. Alone and forgotten in a country most couldn't find on the map. Sons, husbands, brothers. All dead, all forgotten.

Virgil stood on knees shaking and weak. He went to the washbasin and wiped himself down. Then he dressed as quickly as possible and ran from the small room.

The sun was barely coming up in the east. He still shook, but he managed to get his squad car started and drove to Betty's Diner. The lights were on, but no customers had shown up yet. Hopefully, she'd have some coffee brewed.

He walked in and the waitress took one look at him and shoved a cup of steaming coffee in front of him. He cradled it with his hands and stared into the darkness.

The waitress didn't speak and went about opening the restaurant for the daily business. Betty walked behind the counter, took one look at him and moved on. She'd seen him like this before. He didn't want to talk. He just had to get out of that room and into something normal.

No need for company. He just had to wait for the feelings, the pain and the hurt to fade away. And it would eventually. It always did. In the meantime, he worked to try to clear his head. The dream wasn't real, they'd fought back the Germans even though they were out-numbered and eventually help did arrive.

Then he demanded his company be off the front lines for a week to rest and to settle their nerves. The commander didn't like it and he threatened to court-martial Virgil, but he didn't care. Those fighting men deserved a break from killing.

Virgil sat at the counter on a round stool staring at nothing. The coffee warmed his insides, but it did little else. A few customers came in and spoke, but he could only nod. It'd take him a while to return to normal. Once that happened, he'd be okay.

Feeling stronger, he stood and stepped out the door. Cora, holding Jack and Tommy's hand, walked toward the school. She looked so pretty today. The glowing smile on her face assured him she was okay. Then she bent down and said something to Jack. He and Tommy laughed. Pal trotted briskly beside them, tiny barks filling the air.

Virgil smiled at the happiness they shared. From behind, little Ronnie with his pathetic haircut came running toward them. Cora bent down and hugged him tightly to her chest. He was out of breath and chattering like a normal kid. With the three boys in tow, Cora, the ex-con, a woman guilty of trying to murder someone, a person some felt not fit to live in this town, went about her business with a grateful smile on her face.

She was better than all of them.

People like her were the reason he'd fought. So everyone could walk down the streets of America and fear nothing because he'd fought evil and his men had won.

CHAPTER SEVEN

Seeing Ronnie's smiling face lightened Cora's mood. She didn't want to think what might have happened in his house yesterday. However, today he seemed fine.

Jack waved. "Hi, Sheriff."

Cora glanced across the street as Virgil walked from Betty's Diner. Even from her distance she noticed he looked tired, tense and somber.

He mustered up a smile. "Morning. Have a good day in school."

Cora found his coldness unusual and not like him at all. Had something happened? He seemed different in some way. Strange and aloof.

Without another word, he slid into his black and white and drove away. She felt a little let down that he hadn't said anything to her, but then she reminded herself that's exactly the way she preferred the whole situation.

Besides, once Virgil learned the whole truth, he wouldn't be interested in her anyway. Still, not even a wave in her direction stung. Brushing it all off, she walked the children to school and boldly went up to Miss Potter with a pleasant greeting.

The teacher fudged a smile, but Cora left the boys and headed off to work at the dry cleaners. When she entered the shop, the girls ran to greet her.

Nell walked up and hugged her tightly. "We're so glad you're back."

Cora basked in their warm friendship, especially after the coldness from the sheriff earlier. "It's wonderful to have a job and be back with you ladies."

Helen had a sheet of paper she waved in the air. "We've ordered new supplies, but there aren't any good dryers on the market yet, so we'll still have to dry clothes the old fashioned way. But the new dry cleaning machine will be a great improvement."

Cora smiled. "You've accomplished so much already."

Nell moved closer. "I heard old Bart got caught selling bootleg whiskey out of the back shed and he's going to prison."

Ma Baker shook her head. "I knew all along that man wasn't worth a dime."

Helen said, "We're all lucky we have our jobs and everything worked out okay."

Cora went to her ironing station. "I'm just grateful Bart finally got what he deserved."

Nell chuckled. "And we don't have to do anything besides our jobs to keep working."

Helen turned over the open sign. "I'm glad things are settled."

"And I like Mr. Bridges," Nell said. "He's a nice man."

Their first customer came in and the day became busier as time went on. Everyone who came through the door wanted the latest update on Bart. When Cora finally finished and headed to pick up Jack from school, Maggie came by. "I'll fetch the kids."

"Are you sure?"

"I'm going to be in town anyway." Maggie laughed. "I saw Ronnie's haircut."

"Virgil isn't a barber. When Warren saw him, he had a fit. Even came to my house threatening me."

"Did you tell Virgil?"

"No, I haven't seen him." She didn't want to explain the distance she felt between them.

"Then go to his office."

"I'll tell him the next time I run into him."

"You better not wait too long. Nobody knows what Warren's capable of."

"With the break in at my house, and the arrest of Bart, he's been pretty busy lately."

Maggie touched her arm. "Think of Jack."

While Maggie set off for the school, Cora walked to the town square and into Virgil's office.

John greeted her. "Hello, Miss Williams. How can I help you?"

"Is Sheriff Carter here?"

"Yes, ma'am, he's in his office. Just a moment."

She waited outside, nervous and wondering if she was here because of Warren or her desire to see Virgil and make sure everything was all right between them.

Virgil appeared in the doorway. He was handsome as ever, but he hadn't shaved today, he looked disheveled, sad and strictly professional. "Can I help you?"

He didn't invite her into his office. She wondered what she'd done wrong. While Sunday he appeared happy to be with her, today he became distant and withdrawn.

She noticed John listened intently. "I just wanted to let you know that Warren Hayes came to my house last night and threatened me."

"What'd he say?"

"I didn't want to bring this to your attention, but Maggie insisted."

"Miss Williams, what did he say?"

So, they were back to Miss Williams.

He was angry and probably annoyed she'd come to him with the slightest provocation. She turned to go. "I'm sorry to have bothered you."

Thankful to be out the door, she turned for home. Tears threatened but she didn't know why. Why did she care that he was brushing her off acting like he didn't care? Did she want him to care?

She just wanted to get home. Home to the safety of closed doors and Jack. She looked behind her, half expecting him to come after her, but he didn't. The sidewalk behind her was empty. If she was hoping for dramatics, it hadn't happened.

She gratefully arrived home and started dinner. Her feelings had been hurt by Virgil's indifference and his eyes appeared empty and cold. What had happened? What had she done?

Trying to push her thoughts aside, she called Jack for dinner. While they ate, she enjoyed him reliving his day. Miss Potter had been very nice and the little redheaded boy had even joined him, Tommy and Ronnie at their table for lunch.

So, she hadn't ruined Jack's school life with her outspoken silliness. She was glad. With all the mistakes she had to make amends for, she didn't need another.

Jack later recounted how Ronnie's haircut had created quite a sensation with several boys wanting the same style. Cora could only laugh.

After dinner, she cleaned the table and allowed Jack to run and play for a while before bedtime.

She went to the trash and waved to Maggie across the street. "Did you talk to Virgil?"

"No, he's too busy. I'll mention something the next time I see him."

Maggie frowned. "Don't let it slide."

About that time Warren came out of his house and staggered down the sidewalk toward town. She quickly glanced to where the boys were playing. Jack and Tommy shoved Ronnie behind a tree and stood in front of it, trying to look innocent.

It amazed her that even small children learned quickly how to protect those they cared about. Warren stepped off the curb and fell in the middle of the street. That's when the police car pulled up and stopped in the middle of the road.

Virgil got out of the car and picked up Warren and put him in the back seat. He looked at her, his hand on the open door. "Can you see to Ronnie tonight? Warren is going to spend the night in jail for being drunk and disorderly."

Cora nodded and the three boys ran toward her. Ronnie wrapped his skinny arms around her legs and buried his face. "Come inside. Have you had dinner?"

Ronnie shook his head.

"Well, let's find you something to eat."

She took the young boy and Jack inside and scrambled a few eggs and cut a slice of ham and allowed Ronnie to eat his fill. His hair looked horrible, but at least tonight she knew he would be safe.

She had Jack and Ronnie stay in the rest of the night and play board games because she feared Warren might manage to get out and come for Ronnie.

She expected Virgil to lock Warren up and then perhaps come to see how Ronnie was, but she didn't see him that night. After the boys were tucked in bed, she took a cup of coffee and sat on the newly repaired steps.

After a few minutes she went inside and got ready for bed. She'd put on her gown and had turned back the covers on her bed when a soft knock sounded at the door.

She pulled back the curtain and saw Virgil's tall frame. She cracked the door. "I'm ready for bed. What do you want?"

"I don't want to come in. I just came to apologize. I'm not myself today."

"I understand. Everyone has an off day." She looked at him. "Anything I can do to help?"

"No, it's best I deal with this myself."

"Okay. I hope you feel better tomorrow."

He tipped his hat. "I'll see you."

"Is Mr. Hayes locked up?"

"Yes. He's screaming his head off, but he's safely behind bars. I'll let him go tomorrow after a stern warning."

"Thank you and good night."

Cora closed the door and wondered what had made Virgil so sad. Had something happened in his family? She couldn't help solve a problem she knew nothing about. If she could help, she would, but he wouldn't allow her in, so Cora went to bed.

She lay awake most of the night. She'd been careful to check Ronnie for bruises when she bathed him and he appeared okay. Warren was in jail and she had her job back, so why wasn't her mind uncluttered enough to go to sleep?

She got out of bed for a drink of water when she noticed something. Peeking around the curtains, she saw Virgil sitting in his squad car, sound asleep.

Strange.

She felt compelled to wake him and offer the couch, but she didn't want to put up with the gossip, even though, as Virgil said, they were adults. Jack didn't need the backlash.

What was going on and how would it affect their lives?

CHAPTER EIGHT

Virgil hadn't been able to shake his demons all day. He'd been restless, nervous, and unusually jumpy. He chose safety over anything else and stayed close to his office doing paperwork.

Gene McKinnon called from Joplin about Bart, but now at the end of the day, Virgil could barely remember what he'd said. Instead, the day passed in a blur. Bits of his dream kept stealing back to clutter his memory. The exploding shells, the gunfire, men screaming. All the sounds dogged him like a bloodhound.

He imagined John had gotten used to his unusual behavior and knew when to leave him alone since he was out of the office most of the day. Anything that came in, John was quick to take on and leave the office.

Virgil felt bad, but there wasn't much he could do about it. By the time Cora showed up at his office, his jaws were sore and his nerves stretched like a rubber band. He'd been short and unkind to her and he'd like to make it up, but he'd be better off leaving her alone.

Times like now, he didn't know how he'd react to things and he didn't want to upset her further.

However, he had to take care of Warren. If anything happened to Cora, Virgil would never be able to live with the consequences. He couldn't be burdened further.

His original plan had been to visit Warren's home and give him a final warning. Instead he'd found the man sprawled out in the street, drunk out of his mind.

Virgil had brought him back to the station and locked Warren up, after banging his head against the bars a time or two. Served the bastard right for picking on a little kid.

Now, late into the night, he sat outside Cora's house and rested his head against the back of his seat. Eyes closed he keep his mind busy. Tonight he wouldn't sleep. No, he couldn't suffer the nightmares two nights in a row.

So, he stayed outside her house and took comfort in knowing that all those inside were safe and his bad memories would diminish and he could eventually fall asleep undisturbed.

The sun and a stinging pain in his neck woke him the next morning just as the sun rose. Inside Cora's, the lights were on and signs of activity were emanating from the house.

Not wanting to get caught lingering in front of her house, he started the motor and prepared to drive away. Cora stuck her head out the door.

"There's coffee ready."

She went back inside and a smile tugged at the corners of his lips. Turning off the engine, he went inside and greeted everyone. Cora was already dressed in a pretty, forest green dress, her hair elegantly pulled behind her ears.

Jack and Ronnie were spick and span. Hair combed the best it could be, they sat at the breakfast table eating bacon and toast with tall glasses of milk next to them.

His plate sat in front of his usual chair. She'd tossed in a few eggs for him and they all ate among comfortable chatter. Jack talked about a party at school that Cora would have to make cupcakes for and Ronnie talked about an art project he'd been doing.

Pal sat by the kitchen sink, waiting to escort everyone to school and work. "Hurry, boys, we don't want to be late."

"How would you boys like a ride to school in the police car?"

He smiled at Cora and for a moment she looked as if she might object then she smiled and nodded.

"Can Tommy come too?"

"We'll pick him up. But first, you have to finish your breakfast. We leave in five minutes."

As the boys gobbled down their meal, Cora looked at him. "Thank you. That's very kind."

"I...I owe you an apology."

She shrugged. "I'd rather you tell me what's wrong than to apologize."

He stood. "Maybe someday." He put on his hat. "Come on, Pal. You get to go for a ride too."

The boys were already in the car and Pal jumped in beside them with his head out the window. Maggie waved and he pulled out and headed for the school.

Cora would have plenty of time to straighten up and walk to work. He would've offered to take her to work, but he didn't want to talk about his nightmares. He would someday, but not now. Now with the memory so fresh.

He dropped the kids off and took Pal to the office with him. The dog found a comfortable place in the corner and laid down for a nap.

John squatted down and petted the mutt. "Who's this?"

"That's Pal, Jack's dog."

"He the one that bit Bergman?"

"We think so."

John patted him on the head. "Good boy."

"Warren still sleeping it off?"

"Yeah, I haven't heard a peep out of him."

Virgil went into the area where the jail cell stood. "Time to wake up, Warren."

He mumbled something undistinguishable.

"You need to get up and go home."

Warren rubbed his head and sat on the edge of the bunk. His eyes were bloodshot and he stunk like an empty bottle of whiskey. "What time is it?"

Virgil unlocked the cell door and pushed it wide. "Still morning."

John came in and offered Warren a cup of coffee then turned to leave.

Warren blew on the hot brew while glaring at Virgil. "Why'd you lock me up?"

"You were drunk and laying in the street. That's a hazard to you and the public."

"You're just getting even because I threatened to go to the judge."

"Someone call me?" Judge Garner's voice carried inside the small jailhouse. He went back to the cell and stared at Warren. "What happened here?"

"Sheriff locked me up because I told him he had no right to cut my son's hair. And he ain't."

Judge looked at Virgil. "Why'd you cut Ronnie's hair?"

"He'd spent the night at Jack's. Warren was so drunk he didn't even bother to find out where the kid was. She gave him a bath. The next day she was going to trim his hair a little because it hung in his eyes."

Judge looked at Warren. "Nothing wrong with that, Hayes." Judge poured himself a cup of coffee. "Looks like Virgil was doing you a favor."

"He butchered my son's hair. He looks like a freak!"

"He's right there. I did botch the job pretty bad. Then when I saw it was beyond repair, I went to Leonard and had him open the shop to fix Ronnie's hair." He glared at Warren. "Which cost double."

"I didn't tell you to spend a dime, you damn, arrogant son of a bitch. You think you can just take over my kid."

"I felt sorry for a little boy who gets the hell beat out of him every time his worthless old man gets drunk and decides it's time for a little discipline."

"The damn Bible says, 'spare the rod, spoil the child' for Christ sakes."

Judge leaned against the wall, enjoying his coffee. "Funny, Warren, but I bet that's probably the only verse you remember from the good book."

"You taking his side?"

"I'm telling you the sheriff has taken an interest in your child, and a show of goodwill on his behalf, no matter how bad it may go, isn't against the law."

"Why not?" Warren raised his voice and pointed his finger. "How come he's allowed to stick his nose where it doesn't belong?"

"Because his actions were neighborly. He meant the boy no harm."

"That ain't right!"

The judge came to the cell and gripped the iron bars. "What's not right is you beating a little boy until you leave marks on him. That is against all the rules of mankind. There isn't a legal ban against child abuse, but that doesn't make it acceptable."

"Child abuse?" Warren screamed. "What kind of bullshit is that? There ain't no abuse going on in my house and nobody can prove there is."

"Go home, Warren, and try to stay sober."

"Go to hell, all of you. You keep sticking your nose in my business and I'm going to leave this damn town."

Virgil slumped down in a nearby chair. "Where are all the nice people in this town? Why do all the crazy ones end up in here?"

"Virgil you have a good heart. Warren just doesn't see that."

"You know, Cora Williams is so nice to Ronnie, you'd think Warren would be happy someone feeds the boy, gives him a bath, mends his clothes." Virgil ran his fingers through his hair. "Instead he acts so indignant that someone actually cares."

Judge Garner put his cup down and headed for the door. "We all depend on this office to keep the peace and keep those who harm others away from law-abiding citizens. No one said it would be easy."

"It's damn hard."

The judge stood at the door. "Walk me to my office."

Virgil came to his feet and put on his hat. As soon as the door was closed, Garner turned to him. "What's this about Bart?"

"John and I found a shed full of illegal whiskey. I suspect he's been selling it to a guy in Kansas."

"The FBI stepped in?"

"Yes, because alcohol is federal."

"I got a call from Gene McKinnon's office."

"I requested he take the case."

"His boss is concerned."

That didn't make any sense. Gene's boss should give him a commendation for doing his job. He has a great federal agent who risks his life to bring bad guys like Bart to justice.

Virgil stepped off the curb next to the judge. "I don't understand."

"According to the office in Langley in Virginia, Bart's a lot bigger fish than you two had first imagined."

He stopped, his brows furrowed. "Bart?" Virgil chuckled. "We are talking about that piece of shit that forced himself on his employees?"

"Yeah, the same one who beat young Adeline Shoemaker."

"What's he in to?"

"It seems his partner sang like a bird. This case may be bigger than you thought."

"No kidding."

"Gene's supervisor said you may be called to testify. Also, there are a few things he wants you to investigate."

"Okay, just tell me what you want me to do."

"Come with me to my office. I don't want word getting out."

CHAPTER NINE

Cora had baked a cake the night before and brought it to work to share with her co-workers. They needed to celebrate the fact that Bart wouldn't be making sexual demands on them anymore.

Helen saw her first. "What do you have there?"

Cora held out the plate. "I baked a chocolate cake. I thought we'd all enjoy it with our lunch today."

Nell came by. "That's decorated real pretty, Miss Cora. You learn to bake like that in prison?"

Cora stopped and her heart stammered. The girls hadn't talked openly about her time behind bars, but now she realized it needed to be out in the open. At least part of it. "I did learn to bake while I was there."

Nell pointed to the cake. "They had fancy food like this?"

"Oh, not for the inmates. But the warden was always having important guests for dinner because he wanted to run for public office someday." Cora put the cake on their small lunch table. "They assigned me to the kitchen and I was placed under a colored lady named Ellie Fry, who once worked in a fancy New York restaurant."

Nell looked at the cake with its swirling frosting. "I bet she could make some good food."

"For her, cooking was an art."

Ma Baker lifted her arm and pranced around. "She must've been an artist."

Cora laughed. "She was very talented. She taught me everything I know."

Helen took four saucers down from the cabinet. "I think you need to let us be the judge of that. And to do that, we need to sample your cake. Should we wait until lunch?"

They all declined and Cora received the honor of slicing a piece for each of them. She'd hoped they liked her favorite creation, but she never imagined their reaction would be so favorable.

Nell put a forkful in her mouth and closed her eyes. Slowly withdrawing the utensil, she savored the cake. "I swear I've never tasted anything so delicious in all my life."

"Then you've never eaten Naomi's chocolate cake. She works for my parents and she refuses to give up her recipe."

Helen licked the fork. "I agree with Nell, this tastes like heaven."

Cora smiled. "Thank you."

Ma Baker cut herself another smaller piece. "I could eat this all day."

"I'll gladly share the recipe. It's not that hard to make."

Helen put the saucers in the sink. "Good, my husband's birthday is next week and I'd love to make him something that special. You'll also have to show me how to make those fancy swirls."

"All very easy."

They kept busy most of the morning and soon after they had lunch, JJ ran into the dry cleaners. "Miss Cora, please come."

"What's wrong?"

"Little, colored girl is terribly sick."

"Where is Doctor Westley?"

"He's in Joplin. We've called him, but the girl can't wait."

Helen put her hand on Cora's arm. "You go see what you can do. We'll cover here."

Cora ran with JJ to the small but well-cared-for carriage house. The door flew open and a woman in her early thirties stood at the door, a man clutching her shoulders.

"She's in the back bedroom."

Cora followed JJ as they entered a little girl's bedroom. A young girl, no older than seven, lay on the bed. "What's wrong with her?"

The mother sat on the opposite side of the bed. "She's been complaining of stomach pains all morning. I kept her out of school thinking she just had a bellyache, but then she developed a fever."

Cora pressed her palm to the girl's forehead and found it hot. "You need to lower the temperature. We'll need some cool water and a cloth."

The mother ran off to do Cora's bidding.

"Has the doctor been advised?"

"We called him at the hospital in Joplin. He was in surgery and they said he'd leave as soon as possible. We haven't heard anything since then."

Cora brushed back the little girl's hair. "May I check your tummy?"

The girl nodded. "But it hurts."

"I'll be very careful."

She lifted the nightshirt and pressed on the left side of the abdomen and the girl cried out.

Cora looked at JJ. "She has appendicitis. If she isn't rushed to the hospital, I'm not sure she'll make it."

"You're probably right, but it's very hard to get a colored person treatment in the hospital without Dr. Westley."

"She can't wait. Get her to the car and let's take her to the emergency room."

The father bundled up the girl who vomited and appeared close to convulsing. He put her in the back seat of the car. Cradled in her mother's arms on one side, Cora held her hand on the other. The father stepped on the gas and headed for the hospital.

Cora rubbed her forehead. "What's her name?"

"Betsy," her mother's voice trembled. "Betsy Ford." She nodded to the driver. "That's my husband Russell and I'm Ruth." She stretched across and clutched Cora's hand. "I can't tell you how grateful we are."

"Let's hope we get her to the hospital in time."

JJ followed closely behind them.

They pulled up to the emergency entrance of the hospital. Cora ran inside and called to a nearby nurse. "There is a child outside and it appears she's having an appendicitis attack."

The nurse and an orderly grabbed a gurney and ran for the door. They approached the vehicle and carefully removed Betsy from the back seat and wheeled her into the hospital.

Inside, they placed Betsy in a curtained room.

"Where is Dr. Westley?" the nurse asked.

"I'm not sure," Cora replied. "He's been called but he's in Joplin at the hospital there."

A doctor came out and barely glanced at the girl. "That's one of Dr. Westley's patients. Someone call him."

Cora stepped forward. "He's been called, but he's not here at the moment. The girl has a high fever, chills, vomiting, and pain in her lower left abdomen. That would be typical of a ruptured appendix."

The doctor glared at her, a scornful look dressed his wrinkled face. "Who are you?"

"I was just called in by the family."

"Tend to her fever and we'll wait for Dr. Westley."

Cora touched the doctor's arm. "I don't think that little girl has time to wait."

"I don't operate on colored people. Those are Dr. Westley's patients."

She couldn't believe her ears. The little girl's parents and JJ stood off to the side. "Are you refusing this child care based on the color of her skin?"

"I'm telling you that when Dr. Westley arrives, he'll take care of his patient."

"Examine the child, decide what's wrong and fix it. Or I'll turn you over to the Medical Association. I won't stop until you lose your license."

"Just who do you think you are?"

"Someone who took the same oath you did." She glanced at the name tag. *Dr. Adams*. "Do I need to recite it to remind you of your duty to care for those in need?"

Angry, the doctor flipped back the curtain just as the girl convulsed. Cora held her down as the doctor instructed the nurse to get the operating room ready. He glared at her across the girl's sick body.

Cora said, "I'm not asking you to like me, I just want to see the child gets proper treatment, as every human deserves."

They wheeled Betsy out of the room and down the hall. Cora prayed they made it in time.

She joined the family and smiled faintly. "They're taking her into surgery."

The girl's mother clutched Cora's arm. "Will she make it? Did we get here in time?"

"There's no way to tell. Let's just pray they can save her. The important thing is she's being cared for at this time."

The mother glanced at the nurse who'd yet to even approach them. "If you hadn't demanded Betsy be treated, they would've let her die."

Cora put her arm around the grieving mother. "We don't know that. Now is the time for prayer and hope. Not anger."

Cora went to the Nurse's Station. "What floor can the parents wait for their child to come out of surgery?"

"Usually Dr. Westley's patients wait in the side room. When he's done, he comes and talks to them."

Cora pressed her hands on the counter and leaned closer. "Where would the parents of the seriously ill child wait?"

The nurse slammed the metal file. "They stay where they are. Now get away from this station before I call security."

"I truly wish you would call security. And Sheriff Carter while you're at it. And maybe the mayor as well. Perhaps the newspaper would like to hear that a child wasn't cared for in this facility because of the color of her skin."

"You're just a troublemaker."

"No, I'm someone who dedicated years of her life to helping the sick. While my license was taken from me, it doesn't mean I stopped caring." She glanced at the nurse's name tag. "Every morning when you're getting ready for work, remember why you chose this profession, Nurse Hill."

With downcast eyes, the nurse said, "Dr. Adams is operating on the second floor. There's a waiting room up there."

"Thank you very much, Nurse Hill."

Cora walked with the parents to the waiting room. JJ approached her. "Thank you so much for helping my friends. We didn't know where else to go."

"I'm glad I could help."

A colored man walked in and the girl's mother cried out. "Oh, Dr. Westley, Betsy was so sick. We didn't know what to do."

"It's okay. I just talked to Dr. Adams and it appears she's going to be okay."

JJ stepped over. "Dr. Westley, this is Dr. Cora Williams. She's no longer allowed to practice medicine, but today she managed to get the care Betsy needed."

He held out his hand. "For that, I'm in your debt."

"Anytime. But I'm sure Dr. Adams will have plenty to say to the Hospital Administrator."

"I can handle that."

"Then if it's okay with you, now that the little girl is okay, I'd better get back to work."

"I'll gladly drive you, Miss Cora," JJ offered.

Together they turned to leave the hospital. As they stepped from the elevator, Elbert Levy waited with several files in his hand. He stopped and stared at her.

"What are you doing here?"

Cora smiled. "Playing doctor."

That said, they left and went into the parking lot. JJ opened the door for her. "Do you know Mr. Levy?"

"No, not really. He's just making sure I don't try to get a job at his hospital."

"It's not his hospital. He has that job because the people on the council elected him."

"Well, he came to my house and told me not to apply for a job at his hospital. Evidently, my father primed him with a large donation."

"You're kidding. That donation came from your father?"

"I think it might have."

"Levy said he received it because of his dedicated work and innovations. What a liar."

"How did you know about the money?"

"I'm on the council."

"That's good, JJ." She smiled at him. "I've been meaning to come by and thank you for fixing my steps."

"That was my pleasure."

"I can't tell you how much it helped me and Jack. I could never manage a job that complicated and you did a wonderful job."

"I'm a lot like my dad. When I see wood I either want to fix or make something."

"Yet, you became a lawyer?"

"My father always wanted me to be more than him. I only wish I was as good a person."

"He sounds like a wonderful person. I look forward to meeting him and your lovely wife."

They arrived at the dry cleaners and Cora returned to work. "Thank you all for covering for me."

"Is the little girl okay?"

"She's going to be fine. It was her appendix. I'm glad we got her there in time."

Nell came over. "Where was Dr. Westley?"

"He was tied up in surgery in Joplin."

"They let that colored girl in without a negro doctor?"

She smiled. "With a little coaxing."

They all looked up. Bart's wife, Ester, stormed into the dry cleaners.

CHAPTER TEN

As Virgil stood to follow the judge, he got as far as the middle of the street when John stuck his head out and hollered. "Virgil, old man Trenton and Lester Cannon are at it again. They both have guns."

"Hey, Judge, let me take care of this and I'll check in with you later."

"Okay, be careful."

They arrived at that edge of town where Trenton stood with his hunting rifle pointed at Lester's dog, Bully. Nothing like a Mexican standoff to make your day. Lester had his gun pointed at Trenton, cussing like crazy.

Virgil stepped forward. "You two fools put those guns away before you get hurt."

"I warned him about his chicken killing dog. Now I'm gonna shoot that dog."

Lester cocked his Henry rifle. "You shoot my dog, you're gonna die."

"Oh yeah, who says so. I can take you out right where you stand."

Lifting the weapon up, Lester replied, "I was always a better shot than you any day of the week."

Stepping closer, Virgil held up his hands. "Men, let's be mature and put all the guns away. This isn't the way to solve a problem." Virgil had been dealing with these two since he took office. "Lester, you're either going to have to pen that dog up, or someone's going to get hurt."

"Why can't he put his chickens in a pen? They wander all over the place, shitting and scratching."

John stepped forward and nodded. "You should pen those chickens up because a fox is going to get them."

Trenton frowned and lowered his weapon. "I put them in the pen at night. It's during the day his dog kills the chickens."

Cocking his hip and jamming his hands on his hips, Virgil asked, "Have you seen the dog kill a chicken?"

"No, but he's always chasing them around."

"Show me the latest chicken."

They walked over to the dead carcass and Virgil saw immediately this wasn't the work of a dog. It looked more like a cat with the scratches on the dead chicken. He looked around.

"I think me might have a mountain lion or a bobcat in the area."

Trenton shook his head. "I ain't seen one of those in years."

"Don't mean they're not here."

Lester scratched his beard. "That would explain a lot."

Red faced, Trenton shouted, "Like what?"

"Like when you said my dog killed one of your chickens and he was with me the whole day."

"That dog runs wild most of the time. He can't be trusted."

Virgil stepped between the two older men and spread out his arms, splitting them apart. "But if it's a mountain lion, we have bigger problems than a dog."

After searching for an hour, John came across some tracks and called out to the other men. Heads together, they slowly walked alongside the markings. Virgil stopped and knelt down. "These aren't dog tracks. That's a cat."

"It sure the hell is," Trenton remarked. "We'd better find that son of a bitch or else."

Lester patted him on the shoulder. "We'll find him together. In the meantime, you keep your chickens locked up and I'll keep the dog in the house. We don't know how big the cat is. Might be dangerous for all of us."

"I agree."

Lester started walking away. "I'm checking with a few neighbors and see if they've noticed anything."

His neighbor who earlier held him at gunpoint agreed. "Yeah, let's check this out."

Virgil and John drove back into town happy that the dispute had finally been settled.

John shook his head. "Those two have been fighting for years. It's almost strange to see them working together on something."

Virgil shifted gears. "Yeah, I know how you feel."

"We stay mighty busy for a small county."

"Crime is everywhere. Be glad we're not in a big city like St. Louis."

"Speaking of, have you found out anything else about Ted's murder?"

"No, the investigation is pretty hush-hush. They don't want too much information getting out there."

"Afraid someone might decide to check out what's going on in that prison?"

"That's my guess. Of course, we're just speculating. We don't have any information, much less facts."

"Could Gene help you with that?"

"I don't think so because Gene operates under strict rules. It has to have something to do with the government. While there are federal prisons, the Women's Penitentiary in Jefferson City is operated and owned by the state."

John looked out the window. "I don't think they'll ever find out anything there. It's all a covered up."

"Could very well be."

"Does Miss Cora say anything about what went on in there?"

"Not a single word and I'm not asking. They could kill her if word got out that she was talking."

"Yeah, if they'd murder a guard, what would keep them from snuffing out an ex-con?"

Virgil looked at his deputy, his mouth tight. "I would."

At the office, Virgil checked in then went back to Judge Garner's office and closed the door. He offered Virgil a seat and moved to the chair behind his desk.

"What's going on, Judge?"

"It appears Bart's been up to a lot more than bootlegging."

"I don't understand. He basically ran the dry cleaners for his father-in-law. Then he decided to sell a little hooch on the side."

"No, that's not the whole story and Bart isn't the only one involved."

Virgil leaned back and propped his ankle on his knee. "I'm all ears."

"There's talk and some evidence that Bart was also into bank fraud."

"Excuse me?"

"Yes. Hard to believe, isn't it?"

"Practically impossible."

"You remember Harriet?"

"She just retired and moved to Kansas to be near her sister."

"Nicest little old lady in the county."

"Well, she lived alone on Nash Street ever since I've known her. Rumor is her husband died years ago in some kind of accident."

"That's what I've always heard. She's lived here over twenty years."

Confused as hell, Virgil sat up. "That sounds about right."

"And between her and Bart they stole nearly seventy-five thousand dollars over the last five years."

"The hell, you say. How do you know that?"

"When Harriet retired I'm sure she took great pains to make sure she covered all their tracks. However, they didn't plan on Bart losing his job, too."

"Bart's job at the dry cleaners?"

"That's how they were laundering the money."

"So Bart was cleaning more than clothes?" Virgil leaned forward, propping his elbows on his knees. "How did you find all this out?"

"Bank manager noticed something strange when he went over the books."

Letting out a breath, Virgil thought he'd heard everything now. "They had been siphoning out money."

"Exactly."

"Can he prove it?"

"That's part of the problem."

"I can tell you right now, you'll never get Bart to confess to anything like that. Even with facing a stiff sentence."

"The troubling thing is the bank manager, Dale Kerr, and Gene's boss think there is a third person involved."

"Who?"

"Don't know yet. Can you go talk to Harriet?"

"I can, but I can do little more than that. She's living in Kansas now. It'll be up to the Police Chief there."

Judge pointed at him. "No, the crime was committed here, in your county. That puts it in your lap."

Letting out a deep breath, Virgil stood. "I guess I can drive over there and speak with her. But first I'm going to the bank and I'm calling Gene. I won't step into a situation I don't know anything about."

"I know you'll do your homework. I have faith in your ability to get to the bottom of things."

"If Harriet and Bart are in on stealing money from the bank, who could be the third person?"

"I don't know and the FBI doesn't have a clue, either. I'm shocked to find Harriet and Bart partnering up. I didn't think they even knew each other."

"You know, if Bart were smart, he would've worked hard and old man Bridges would've made sure he did well. Now, he's lost his job, his family, and will probably spend a lot of time in the slammer."

Virgil wondered how all this happened right under his nose. While he'd never cared for Bart, Harriet was always pleasant and kind. Obviously the bank manager thought so too or he wouldn't be out seventy-five thousand dollars.

Virgil also wondered where she and Bart had hidden the money. What did they plan to use it for? And who was the third person? Could it be the bank manager? Was he guilty? But if so, why would he bring it to the FBI's attention?

None of it made any sense and his job was to get to the bottom of the problem. While the FBI had control of the case, he had to find out as much as he could in his county.

Virgil liked working with Gene, but he needed to know what the other man knew. If they were going to work together, information sharing was a must.

Garner shook his head. "This is sure a mess."

"I wish we'd found out sooner. Why didn't the banker keep better tabs on the money he was responsible for?"

"I think he was too busy with his secretary."

"Louise?"

"That's what the FBI has turned up. It appears they meet regularly at the Motor Inn on the edge of town."

Virgil smacked his leg. "Damnnit, am I living in another world. All this stuff going on in my county and I don't have even the slightest idea?"

The judge held up his hands. "I didn't know anything either. I was thinking of asking Harriet if she'd like to have dinner one night before she retired. That's how big a fool I am."

"It's just all too much. First Cora moves here, it gets confirmed that Bart is sexually intimidating his female employees, then we learn he's into bootlegging. Now you sit there and tell me him and a nice, little, old lady have also been embezzling from the bank."

Judge Garner shook his head. "It's shocking."

"Things are completely out of hand around here. While I'm settling disputes between men over chickens and a dog, serious crimes are being committed right under my nose."

He stood and paced. "Here I've been accosted by the citizens because an ex-con moved in, everyone's getting all riled up because Carl gets drunk and causes a little ruckus, and here there's a major crime spree in our midst."

"I think we might just have a few bad apples we need to take care of and we'll be fine."

"Lord, what a mess." He leaned over the judge's desk. "Do you think I can hire an extra deputy until all this settles down?"

The judge narrowed his eyes. "I don't know what the council will think of that."

"Well, I'd appreciate you bringing it up. John and I are on duty practically twenty-four hours a day. It'd be best if we could keep regular hours."

"I agree and I'll see what I can do. It might only be part-time."

"I appreciate any help you can get me."

"I feel bad for Ester. She never did anything in her life to deserve this."

"We don't always get what we deserve."

CHAPTER ELEVEN

Cora left the dry cleaners to go pick the boys up from school when a man drove up to the curb next to her and got out of his car. He came around toward her, anger brightening his face.

"Are you Cora Williams?"

Stunned, she backed away. "Yes, why?"

"Did you come to the hospital today with a young colored girl?"

"Yes, she was gravely ill."

He shoved back his hat, put his fists against his bulging waist, and said, "My name is Dr. Janson. I'm head physician of the hospital. My understanding is you came today demanding a colored child be cared for."

Insulted, she tightened her jaw. "I don't know that I actually *demanded* anything, but the child could've died."

"We have strict policies about the care of our patients. Dr. Westley is well aware of how things work. I won't allow someone who's been discharged from the American Medical Association to come into my hospital and start shoving people around."

"Not even to save a child's life?"

He ripped off his hat and smacked it against the side of his leg. He exposed a balding head with a small dusting of light-colored hair surrounding his head. "That's not a decision for you to make."

"Who makes the call, doctor? Which idiot at your hospital plays God? If you think for one minute I'll stand here and take a dressing down from a person so narrow-minded he'd rather put a patient's life in danger than disrupt the policies set in place, you can think again."

Doctor Janson stepped closer. "You'll do as I say or I'll..."

"You'll what? Let the citizens of this town know what a poor excuse for a human being you are?" She turned away. "Then go ahead."

Anger seeped out of her pores, making her want to slug the pious chump. It was difficult to believe that today a little, colored girl getting treated at a local hospital could cause such a disturbance.

The boys were just running down the stairs when she crossed the street, little Ronnie pulling up the rear as usual. Miss Potter walked toward her. Cora realized now would be a good time to apologize to the teacher for her rudeness last Friday.

"Good afternoon, Miss Williams."

"Hello, Miss Potter."

"I wanted to let you know that Jack's doing wonderfully in school. He's such a well-mannered little boy."

Cora touched Miss Potter's arm. "That's so kind of you to say. I want to tell you how sorry I am for my rudeness last week."

"Miss Williams, I teach the children to be polite and to give people the benefit of the doubt. I wasn't practicing what I preach and I'm sorry."

"That's okay, let's put it behind us."

"I agree."

They looked at the boys playing. Miss Potter waved to several other parents. "You know, I worry about little Ronnie."

Cora caught Ronnie running out of the corner of her eye. "I know exactly how you feel. I try to do the best I can, but his father is so unreasonable."

Miss Potter turned away. "And so drunk most of the time."

"I guess you noticed his haircut?"

"I did and while it's not the most flattering cut I've seen, at least it's clean and not hanging in his eyes."

"Mr. Hayes became enraged at the sheriff."

"I wonder if we're not wise to call in the authorities."

"I've thought about that many times myself, but I'd hate for little Ronnie to be taken to an orphanage. He's such a good-natured little boy."

"He tries really hard in school, but there is so much against him. He's not always clean, he's often hungry, and fear follows him around like a shadow."

"I see all that. I feed him every chance I get. I make sure he has a lunch, but sometimes Mr. Hayes keeps the boy in the house for days at a time. I worry so much."

"Can't the sheriff do something?"

"He arrested Mr. Hayes a couple of nights ago, but I don't think he has a strong enough reason to keep him locked up."

"Maybe it's time the women of this town do something."

"What?"

"We'll get our heads together. Maybe we can save Ronnie yet."

Cora called the boys and headed home. She had no idea what Miss Potter had in mind, but she'd do about anything to help Ronnie. Tonight, so he'd be sure to get supper, she'd planned to cook a quick meal of ground beef, tomato sauce and macaroni.

With bread, corn and leftover chocolate cake, she felt sure Ronnie would at least go to bed with a full tummy. While the two boys were playing in Maggie's yard, Cora quickly went about getting dinner ready.

The sheriff appeared at the back door. "Come in," she called.

He walked in wearing his uniform and looking more handsome by the day. She'd had gotten to the point that the minute she saw him her heart acted all funny and she suddenly had the urge to smooth her hair and pressed her dress. She was as bad as a school girl.

"How's your day going?"

She smiled and waved him to the kitchen table. "First, do you want to stay for dinner?"

"I'd love to."

"Okay, it's going to be quick. I never know when Mr. Hayes is going to call Ronnie in and I want to make sure he gets dinner."

"That's fine. Your cooking is wonderful and it beats the heck out of eating at Betty's Diner."

She looked back at him. "You looked worried."

"I spent most of the day with the judge. It appears we have a crime wave here in Gibbs City."

She chuckled. "Really? Someone stealing milk deliveries?"

"No, it appears Bart and the ex-bank teller, Harriet, might've been involved in a theft at the bank."

"Didn't Maggie mention her job was going to be coming open?" She turned around, surprised. "A robbery in our little bank?"

"Yes."

"The one Mr. Kerr works at, where he makes those funny snorting noises, twitches his tiny mustache and constantly adjusts his glasses?"

"The same."

She turned her head and laughed into the bend of her arm. "You're kidding?"

He let out a tired breath. "I wish I was. This is enough to make me want to pull my hair out."

She sat next to him. "I'm sorry, Virgil. It just seems we live in such a small town, who'd imagine."

"I think that was the point."

"And Bart?" She stood and went to the cabinet for plates and glasses. "He is no doubt a rotten rat. But I didn't think he was smart enough to pull off a bank heist."

"The FBI thinks they've been at it for years. A little here and there. Never large sums of money. Nothing to bring attention."

"Maybe that's why Bart guarded the cash register so closely."

"The money went through the dry cleaners. It's called laundering."

"Are you serious?"

"Yes I am and you have to promise to keep quiet about all this until the case is built against the two. No womanly gossip."

She frowned. "You know I don't gossip."

"I do, but just an extra word of caution. I don't even know how many people this will involve."

She set the table. "I'm sorry. It sure makes your job a lot harder."

"I asked the judge to put hiring another deputy to the council."

"The good thing is Bart's in jail. Since Harriet is older, I doubt she will give you too much trouble."

"There is a third person we know nothing about."

"Oh my, that's scary."

"I'm going to Baxter Springs tomorrow. Maybe Harriet will have something to add."

"Let's hope so. I know you'll love putting this behind you."

"It's pretty trying." He cleared his throat. "While I was in the judge's office, Dr. Janson came in complaining about you taking a young, colored girl to the hospital and demanding she be cared for."

She turned to face him. "I demanded nothing. Nor should I have to. A doctor can't refuse anyone treatment."

"I agree with that creed, but I guess you shook things up by bringing the child to the hospital without Dr. Westley."

"He was in Joplin. Should the parents just stand by and let their child die because there isn't a colored physician to do the surgery?"

"Of course not. I think you did the right thing." He held up his finger. "And so did Judge Garner. He told the pompous ass to think about what he was saying."

"Good, the procedures in the hospital need to be brought up before the citizens because no one would let an innocent child die because of color."

"The judge called the mayor and they plan to meet tomorrow to discuss the matter."

"Will you call Ronnie and Jack in? Dinner is ready."

The boys rushed to wash their hands and get to the table. They were both pleased that the sheriff would be joining them. Neither boy could stop talking. Cora wondered how they managed to get any food into their mouths.

After the boys cleaned their plates, she brought out the leftover chocolate cake from the dry cleansers. The boys were delighted and if Virgil's big eyes were any indication, he couldn't wait to sink his teeth into the confection.

She poured the boys extra milk and coffee for her and Virgil. The boys gobbled down the cake and the milk disappeared in a matter of seconds. "Can we be excused?" Ronnie asked. "We found a big chunk of coal to draw with and we're playing four square."

"Okay, but you both have to come in for the night soon."

They ran out the door with Pal right behind them, now that he'd completely healed.

Virgil laughed. "Those two have so much energy."

"Maggie and I were talking about that. These three boys could play until they dropped."

"They're good children."

"You're right. I'm so lucky to have them." She glanced at Virgil, her cheeks warm. "I know I don't have Ronnie, but I have Jack and I'm so thankful."

"Would you take Ronnie if you could?"

"Oh, my goodness, yes. In the blink of an eye. I'd just love to give him a warm, safe environment and a family that loves him."

"I don't see that happening, but I wish it would. Ronnie needs someone to care for him."

"Miss Potter mentioned something today after school, but I don't know what she has in mind."

He stood and together they cleaned the table and washed the dishes.

Cora asked, "Does Ronnie have an aunt or any family?"

"No, I checked when his grandmother died. I knew then that Warren wouldn't want or be able to care for the child."

"I'll just continue to do what I can. I'm not fighting with Mr. Hayes again because Ronnie pays for that. But, I am going to ask if I can see that he gets back and forth to school."

"I doubt he'll object to that unless he thinks I'm in on it."

"He's mad at you for putting him in jail?"

"Yes. But most people are angry once they wake up and realize they've been put behind bars."

"I wish there was more for Ronnie." She glanced out the window and saw Mr. Hayes staggering out of his house. He looked around, no doubt trying to find Ronnie. "Stay here."

Cora walked across her yard and then the street to where Ronnie's father stood. "Mr. Hayes I was wondering if it was okay if Ronnie spent the night with Jack?"

"You need to mind your own business."

"I realize that, but since it's getting so late, won't you let Ronnie come to our house. I promise I'll get him to school on time tomorrow."

He staggered, scratching his head. In a mind muddled with liquor, Cora had no idea what rattled around in there, but he squared his shoulders and nodded. "Since you asked so nicely, I give my permission for Ronnie to spend the night with Jack." He pointed a finger at her. "You be sure he gets to school on time."

Cora put her hands together and smiled. "Oh, I promise."

"Okay then. Good night."

Mr. Hayes turned around and went back into his house, leaving her as baffled as if she'd been transported into a foreign land. Not waiting for him to change his mind, she headed back home.

Earl stuck his head out the door. "You okay, missy?"

"Yes, Earl. How are you?"

"Waiting for you to do some baking or did you quit."

"No, I baked a chocolate cake. I think there's a piece left. Would you like that with a cup of fresh coffee?"

He moved rather quickly for a man needing a cane to assist him. "I love chocolate cake. Wanda made the best in the world, so we'll have to see how you did."

"Of course, I understand."

She opened the door as Virgil poured the coffee.

Earl looked at him. "What'd you move in without telling anyone?" Her neighbor sat down. "Every time I come over here I see your ugly face. Don't you have a home?"

Virgil laughed good-naturedly. "I practically live in a closet down at the station, so if you think I'm going to stay away, you've got another think coming."

"Getting sweet on my missy, aren't you?"

Her cheeks were probably as red as a rose. "Earl, that's impolite."

Her neighbor laughed. "He ain't denying nothing, is he?"

Virgil looked at her, his eyes alight with mischief. "I'm not denying anything."

CHAPTER TWELVE

Next morning Virgil pulled out of his parking space in front of his office, hit route sixty-six and drove straight into the Baxter Springs, Kansas city limits. He knew the police there. Being part of Cherokee County, the town was big enough to have their own Police Chief.

Ken Bishop was close to retirement age. He'd held the office ever since Virgil met him years ago when his father and Ken belonged to the same lodge. They'd take turns meeting in alternating towns.

He stepped into the police station and found Ken sitting at his desk.

Ken stood. "Howdy, Virgil. Long time no see."

"Good morning, Ken. I came here to talk to one of your citizens and I felt it only professional to make you aware of the situation."

"What's going on?"

"I'm here about Harriet Turner, the bank teller from the bank in Gibbs City who retired to move here to be near her sister."

"She never moved here. And her sister died two years ago."

"She'd told everyone in Gibbs City that she planned to retire here."

"Haven't seen her since the day we buried her sister."

"Wonder where she would've gone?"

"Have a seat. Want coffee?"

"No, thank you, I'm fine."

"Harriet used to come to town occasionally and visit, but the last six or seven years we haven't seen much of her. Then her sister had a stroke. Harriet came here and put her in a nursing home. After that she stopped by maybe once every two or three weeks."

"That's kind of surprising. She always claimed that sister was her only family."

"That's not true either."

"No?"

"She's got a brother who lives in Fairland. Leastways he used to. Haven't seen him in years." Ken stood and pulled up his trousers. "What's going on?"

"The FBI thinks Harriet might have something to do with some missing money."

"Well, I'd say that doesn't sound like her, but you and I know in this business, nothing is as it seems. We run into the strangest stuff."

"You're right."

"Just when we think we know someone, they go and prove us wrong."

"You should know firsthand. I never imagined one of your Police Officers was capable of murder."

"Nobody did, including me." He poured more coffee into his cup. "Biggest shock of my life."

"We just have to stay alert and be ready for anything."

"You're right, Virgil." He took a sip of coffee. "How is the judge?"

"He's fine. He's the reason I'm here. Wants to get ahead of the FBI on this investigation. If there's something we need to know, he doesn't want us to look like a bunch of country bumpkins."

"Smart man."

"I've always thought so." Virgil stood. "You know where I can find her brother in Fairland?"

"I don't. He used to own a small business on the main street there, but I heard he sold out. I don't know what happened after that."

"And no signs of Harriet?"

"No, she's hasn't been around here."

"Okay, well, I'll keep you informed."

"You do that. Good luck."

Virgil was on his way out of town when he drove by the local diner and spotted Gene's car. Deciding it might be time for lunch he pulled over and parked. Gene sat in the back booth of the diner, reading the local paper.

He looked up and smiled when he saw Virgil walking toward him. "What brings you here?"

"Probably the same reason as you."

"I was just going to grab a bite to eat then talk to local law enforcement."

Virgil sat down and picked up the menu. "Save your breath. She's not here and her sister died a couple of years back."

"She gave the bank manager her sister's address."

"We can drive out there, but my guess is Harriet is in the wind."

"I have to admit, I wondered if she'd be stupid enough to stick around here and get caught."

"I thought a lot about all this on the way over and it appeared to me that Harriet didn't have any friends, didn't attend church, didn't shop in town, and besides working in the bank, I never saw her."

"She have a house?"

"She rented a small, one bedroom place. The owner lived in in Joplin. Was his mother's old house. Harriet paid on time, never caused any trouble and stayed to herself."

"Sounds like she just faded into the wallpaper."

"The perfect criminal. No one ever noticed her."

"If Bergman hadn't sung like a canary we honestly wouldn't have had a clue."

"I thought the bank manager told your boss?"

"No, my boss called the banker's boss and they came down and had an audit."

"You think the banker is in on it?"

"I don't know. Like I said, until Bergman said Bart had a bunch of money stashed back from the bank, we didn't know anything."

"Bart's lips still sealed?"

"Yes, and he's hired a lawyer."

"He contacted anyone besides an attorney?"

"No, he's been pretty quiet."

"Okay, well, the judge wanted me to look into a few things for your boss, but I'll let you handle it from here. I don't really have the resources and it's federal."

"Yeah, I've got a partner on vacation right now. On his honeymoon. As soon as he gets back, I think we'll be traveling. You don't mind if I search her place in Gibbs City, do you."

"No, help yourself. I gave it a quick once over, but I didn't disturb anything. She left the place bare as a bone."

Virgil placed his order and turned to look out the big picture window overlooking Main Street. He leaned closer. "Well, I'll be damned."

"What?"

Virgil jump up and ran for the door. "That's Harriet at the Union bus stop."

Both men ran across the street and just as the teller went to step onto the bus, Virgil grabbed her by the arm. Gene flashed his badge to the driver. "FBI, turn off the motor."

"Yes, sir."

Gene looked inside the bus. "Where you headed?" he asked the driver.

"Los Angeles."

"I'm going to need you to find her luggage. She's not going anywhere."

Virgil held Harriet while she tried to squirm her way out of his grasp all the while screaming for them to unhand her. Tired of the struggle, he handcuffed her while Gene found her small, brown and beige checkered suitcase.

There was a lock on it. Gene slammed it with the heel of his boot and it popped off. He flipped open the top and stacks of money were crammed into every cranny.

Gene shoved back his hat and whistled. "That's a lot of money, Miss Turner."

"It's my life's savings."

Virgil came closer. "That's the banks money."

Her eyes narrowed slyly. "That's my money. I worked there for years, putting up with Dale Kerr's nonsense. The foolish way him and the Louise would carry on, it was disgraceful."

"Is that why you took the money? Because he was giving his attention to someone else?"

"I don't care what he does. I'm just glad the home office will find out and his life will be ruined."

"Where did Bart come into play?"

Shock registered in her eyes. "You know about that?" Harriet lowered her head. "He agreed to launder the money so no one would suspect anything. He'd make a daily deposit, I'd adjust the receipt then he'd make a withdrawal at the end of the week."

"Well, you're both going away for a long time, so I hope it was all worth it."

She squared her shoulders. "It will be. Wait until Kerr's wife finds out what he's been doing."

"Wouldn't it have been easier to just tell her yourself?"

"And get a reputation as a gossiper?" Harriet lifted her nose. "Never."

Gene and Virgil looked at each other and shrugged.

Virgil handed Harriet over and tipped his hat. "She's all yours. I'm heading back to Parker County."

Virgil couldn't get over the reason the ex-teller had stolen the money. Love made people do foolish things. His thoughts immediately went to Cora and her soft, brown hair and warm eyes. There was so much to admire about her.

The way she cared for Jack and even Ronnie. She had a kind and giving heart. But she managed to keep it well protected from harm.

He hit Main Street and went to the bank. He'd planned to speak to the banker and possibly notify his supervisor what he'd been up to, but evidently the news traveled faster than he did.

Inside the bank, Dale Kerr was cleaning out his desk. He'd been fired and would not be allowed back in the bank. Virgil introduced himself to the bank president, Harry Stewart, who shook his hand. Stewart had keen, brown eyes, a head of thick light hair, was polite and intelligent.

"I'm glad the money was found. At least most of it. Do you think Mr. Cooper knows where the rest is?"

Virgil rubbed the back of his neck. "I'm not sure. You'll have to check in Joplin with the FBI. Cooper's being held there."

"Okay, I'm staying at a local hotel. I can't stay too long. I'm here to see that Kerr leaves and to find someone who can run the bank until I can find a permanent replacement."

"Well, let me know if I can be of any help. And enjoy our town while you're here."

Virgil went to the dry cleaners to see Cora. He didn't want to disturb her, but thought he'd let the ladies know what was going on at the bank.

"It appears Bart and Harriet were stealing from the bank. Bart and his partner have been arrested, and Mr. Stewart is here from the bank's home office to get things in order."

Ma Baker came closer. "We heard Kerr was having a dalliance with his secretary."

"That's gossip. I don't know if that's true." He didn't want to feed the chatter.

Helen laughed. "And she sits right in the front row at church."

Cora grinned. "You're becoming quite the information gatherer."

"I just wanted you to know that Harriet was in on it and we caught her in Baxter Springs with a suitcase full of money. She thought if she hid out at her sister's abandoned house she'd be safe."

Nell hitched her hip to the counter. "Well, if that don't beat all."

Virgil walked to the door. "Makes me want to go out and investigate everyone in town. You just don't know who you can trust."

Pearl put her hands on her hips. "Old Bart was getting money from bootlegging and stealing from the bank and acted scared to death one of us would take a dime from his cash register."

Virgil shook his head. "He was a devious one all right."

Cora smiled and waved goodbye. Virgil headed to his office. The judge was on his way out of the courthouse when he saw Virgil. Judge Garner called him over.

After relaying all the information, they both figured they'd seen the last of Bart Cooper.

CHAPTER THIRTEEN

Cora grabbed her jacket and headed home from work. Maggie was going to get the boys from school and she wanted a chance to get supper started early.

Never knowing what mood Warren would be in, she wanted to make sure Ronnie had dinner. Pal was happy to see her and she sat on the back porch rubbing his belly until her neighbor came by.

"Evening, Earl."

"Heard about all that ruckus at the bank?"

"Virgil came by the dry cleaners and mentioned it to us. I'm so shocked."

"Can't say I am. I knew the banker was up to no good. Saw him and Louise come out of the hotel once, so I went in and asked the desk clerk. Guy there told me they met regularly."

"That's no reason for Harriet to rob the place."

"If Dale Kerr had been taking care of business, he might've learned the truth a lot earlier."

"I guess you're right. Now he's been fired."

"I saw the bank president when I went by there. Guess he'll be hiring someone to take Kerr's place."

"I wish he'd consider Briggs."

Earl looked across the street at Maggie's. "Why Briggs?"

"His family used to own a big furniture store in Miami and he was their accountant."

"Why's he working in the mines?"

"Because that's the only place hiring."

"He got any schooling?"

"I don't know, but he's as honest as the day is long. He's in charge of the church's money."

"Stands to reason if you can be held responsible for that, you can handle anybody's money."

"Well, I'm sure the bank president will find someone."

"I'll talk to him tomorrow."

Cora stopped. "You know the bank president?"

"Not personally."

"Do you think he'll take your suggestion?"

"More likely he'll tell me to mind my own business."

"Good luck, Earl. And it's very kind of you to consider Briggs."

"Now, don't go patting me on the back. I ain't done nothing and I ain't so sure I can." He turned toward his yard. "'Sides, don't you have anything to bake?"

"I would if I had some apples or maybe some pears, and I can always use pecans."

"Hell fire! You want me to do the baking too?"

She laughed. "If you want."

Cora turned and went inside to fix dinner. She'd meant to invite Virgil over tonight but didn't want to in front of the girls at the dry cleaners. She didn't need any more gossip being spread around about her.

What she really hoped was that Earl would talk to the bank president and he'd consider something for Briggs, even if it were part time, or just until he could find someone qualified.

Soon Ronnie and Jack ran into the house. "Sheriff's car's out front. Is he here?"

Cora looked around. "I don't see him."

She continued peeling potatoes. She'd set out some pork chops and planned to have fried potatoes and corn. Lately she'd always made sure she had extra for Virgil or Earl.

A brisk knock sounded at the back door and the boys ran to let Virgil in.

"Hi," she said. "What to stay for dinner?"

"I'd love to. What are we having? Smells good."

She laughed. "As if you really cared."

"As long as you're cooking, I'm happy. But, I'd like to return the favor. Saturday night can I take you and the boys out for dinner?"

"You mean..."

"I mean, it's time I paid you back for all the food I've been eating here."

Jack ran over. "Can Ronnie come too?"

Virgil squatted down and put his hands on Jack's waist. "If it's okay with his dad."

Ronnie frowned. "I don't think he'll let me go."

"We'll see," said Cora. She hugged Ronnie against her hip. "I'll talk to him and see what he says."

The boys went to Jack's room and she and Virgil shared a doubtful looked. "Warren is just mean enough to say no."

She handed him the plates to set the table. "If we act like it's no big deal he might agree."

"The thing is, you can't tell with that drunk."

"You're right. He's very moody, drunk or sober."

Virgil put his hands on his hips. "When have you ever seen him sober?"

"I'm not sure I have."

"I was going to say. You must've went over there and woke him up or something."

They had dinner and Virgil helped the boys with their baths while Cora mended a pair of Ronnie's pants for school the next day. Soon he'd need a coat and she'd have to purchase it because she doubted he owned one.

She made coffee and pulled a cinnamon loaf out of the oven, sliced it and set it on the table "You know, I never imagined Bart was into so much. His wife came in earlier today."

"What'd she want?"

Cora shrugged. "She claims the reason for the visit was because she wanted to check on all of us and make sure we were all okay."

"That's strange."

"Then she went in Bart's office and went through his drawers like she was looking for something."

"Could be she heard he robbed a bunch of money from the bank and wanted to find it so she could return it."

"I don't know."

"Mr. Bridges would insist that money be returned. He doesn't want a blemish against his name. It's probably killing him that Bart managed to drag his name through the mud."

"Maybe you're right, but what if she wanted that money for herself?"

He laughed. "Cora, you have no idea how rich Mr. Bridges is. She lives in the lap of luxury."

"But, she doesn't have a dime that's hers."

"If she took the stolen money from the bank that wouldn't be hers either."

"I must just be suspicious, but I think she's up to something."

He took a sip of coffee. "Like what?"

"Don't know. But, why come around the dry cleaners? What's there for her? And we all know she's not concerned about us. We're more an embarrassment than something she wants to protect."

Virgil rubbed his face. "I don't know. I'll keep an eye out and see if anything unusual happens. Besides, I'm sure Gene with the FBI has talked to her already."

"Who knows." She rose to get the coffeepot, but Virgil put his hand on her shoulder. "Let me. You've been on your feet all day."

"After work I went to see Betsy Ford. She's still in the hospital, but doing very well. Frank's wife Mae said she'd be coming home tomorrow."

"Doctor didn't run you out of the place?"

"No, but I was hoping he would. This way I could write a letter fast as a grease fire."

She enjoyed her coffee while Virgil filled the sink with soapy water and let the dishes soak. If he wanted to do the dishes, she was tired enough to let him.

A knock sounded on the front door. They exchanged looks. "I'm not expecting anyone."

Virgil wiped his hands and went to answer the door. A man she'd never met stood on the porch. "Hello, Mr. Stewart."

"Good evening, Sheriff. I stopped at your office and Frank the fireman said you'd either be here or at Betty's Diner. I checked there first."

"What can I help you with?"

"Do you have a moment?"

"Yes, come on in." Virgil turned and introduced her. "This is Miss Cora Williams. Cora, this is Harry Stewart, the bank president." Returning his attention to the visitor, Virgil said, "This is her house, if this is law business, we can go to my office."

"No, no, this is strictly personal."

The man looked in his mid-forties with a square body. He was about as big around as he was tall, but he looked professional and a little anxious.

"Won't you have a seat Mr. Stewart? Might I interest you in a cup of coffee?"

"Yes, please. It smells wonderful."

Virgil sat across from him. "We just finished dinner."

"I hope I'm not disturbing you." Cora handed him the coffee and moved to return to the kitchen.

"No, Miss Williams, you're welcome to stay. As a matter of fact you're part of the reason I'm here."

Fear crawled up her back and drew her to a halt. "What? I haven't done anything."

"Oh, no, I don't mean to imply anything is wrong."

Virgil cleared his throat. "Then state your business."

"Mr. Clevenger contacted me today." The banker took a piece of paper from the vest of his suit. "About a Mr. Briggs Cox?"

"What about him?"

"Well, Mr. Clevenger suggested I might talk to him about coming to work at the bank."

Joy circled Cora's heart. "Really?"

"It would only be temporary. You do realize I've fired the bank manager, the head teller and the secretary. There's no one but me working the bank and I'm afraid I can't do everything."

Virgil leaned closer. "I understand. You're in a bind."

"Yes, and until I can rewrite the job descriptions, do interviews, and go through the hiring process, I need some counter help."

"How can we help you?"

"Well, Sheriff, would you give Mr. Cox a good recommendation to come to work for the bank. Our board is demanding honesty and dependability."

Cora tried to hide her excitement. "After what's happened you can hardly blame them."

Mr. Stewart wiped his forehead. "Yes, I do agree with them completely. However, there's no one we can spare in the main office at this time. There was a discussion about closing this branch, but we do have several loyal customers we don't want to lose."

Virgil leaned back. "Briggs is about the most honest person I know. Takes care of the church funds and helps the council with the town budget."

"Do you think he'll consider an offer?"

Cora stood and straightened her dress. "You know he has a job. And if you're only offering a temporary position, he might not be willing to leave the job he has." She cleared her throat. "You know, the whole bird in the hand, thing."

"Well, I don't know. I wasn't informed about him working on the town budget. That's very interesting. And it shows he's used to handling large sums of money."

"He's very thrifty," Virgil added. "When we needed money for a new fire truck, Briggs found it."

"Perhaps, I could hire him full time. Of course, it will all depend on the interview and he will be on probation." Mr. Stewart turned to Virgil. "Sheriff, can you ask him to be at the bank tomorrow before noon?"

"I'll notify him and if he can't make it, I'll drive by and let you know."

Mr. Stewart stood. "I do appreciate and value your opinion. Thank you and good night."

Virgil walked him to the door. When it was shut and locked, Cora ran into his arms and hugged him. "Can you believe it? I'm so excited."

Virgil lowered his head, but Cora quickly stepped out of his reach and put her hands behind her back. "I think you should go tell Briggs."

She knew he wanted to kiss her and she wanted him to, but that would never work out for them. There was so much more to her past than he could imagine. And if he knew even half of it, he'd never set foot back in her house. She'd done things and seen things that no one should ever have to endure.

CHAPTER FOURTEEN

Virgil was disappointed when Cora backed away from him. He knew there were things in her past she didn't want him to know, but he didn't care.

Whatever happened before didn't matter. Not enough to change the way he felt about her. Not enough to make him turn away. Not enough to prevent him wanting his lips on hers so badly he could hardly control his racing heart.

He knocked on Maggie's door and she invited him in. Briggs sat in the living room reading an old Life magazine. "Howdy, Virgil. What brings you out this night? Miss Cora run you off?"

"No," Virgil removed his hat and hung it on the coat tree by the door. "I come with good news."

Maggie put on a pot of coffee. "God knows we can sure use that."

"What's the news?"

"I had dinner over at Cora's and after the boys went to bed and we're having coffee, guess who came knocking on the door."

Briggs shrugged. "I don't know."

"The bank president, Mr. Stewart."

"What's he doing over there?"

"He came to get a recommendation from me."

"For what?"

"For you going to work at the bank."

Briggs looked shocked for a moment then jumped up and ran from the kitchen. "What'd you say?"

"Mr. Stewart is considering offering you a job at the bank."

"I don't have that kind of education."

"I'm sure he probably knows that, but he's lost all his employees and he can't run the bank alone."

"Why'd he think of me?"

"Cora said something to old Earl, and he went down and talked to the bank president."

Maggie put her hand to her lips. "Well, I'll be."

"You think I'll get it?"

"I don't know, but he wants to see you tomorrow at the bank before noon."

"Oh, I'll be there, all right. Maggie, get out my suit."

"It's already out and so is your shoe shining kit."

Briggs walked over and shook Virgil's hand. "Thank you so much, Virgil. You're a true friend."

"You just get that job. I might be asking for a loan someday."

"I'll be there at opening tomorrow."

Maggie held up the coffeepot. "You want a cup?"

"No, I had dinner at Cora's and then we had coffee. I drink anymore I'll be up all night." He walked to the door and got his hat. He turned to his friend. "I'm hoping this works out well for you, Briggs."

"Me too. That's if he doesn't mind hiring a cripple."

"You get around pretty good. And you're smart. It's time you started making money with your brain instead of your back."

They shook hands.

Briggs said, "Let's just hope it works out."

"It will."

Virgil went back across the street. All the lights were out at Cora's so he got in his squad car and drove back to the station.

He got ready for bed but lay awake staring into the darkness. This little room couldn't continue to be his existence. He had to have a place to live and a real home. This had served its purpose for a while but now, he needed to rent or buy a home.

He sat up. Here it was Thursday and he'd yet to start one project he'd promised Cora he'd do. Instead, he'd been showing up at supper time and eating her food. Starting tomorrow he planned to get busy on that house.

There was enough to do to keep him busy for the next month. Besides, he enjoyed being in her company. Maybe too much. He hadn't heard any more from St. Louis about Ted's murder. Maybe they'd found the person responsible. If not, Cora's life could still be in danger.

He hated to pry into her life without her knowing it, but that might be the only way he could find out about her past. Then again, the only person he knew or trusted with that information had been murdered.

Next morning, John arrived bright and early. Virgil had just washed and put on his uniform when the outer door opened.

Virgil heard John making coffee and wondered if he wanted to bother going to Betty's this morning. He stepped out of his room and there were two big cinnamon buns in a wicker basket by a familiar napkin on his desk.

He grinned. "What's this?"

"Hell if I know, but I'm eating one."

A small note was tucked inside. *"Thank you for helping Briggs. Enjoy your day."*

The message wasn't signed, but it had Cora all over it.

"Looks like you and Miss Cora are getting serious."

"No. That's a long ways from the truth. She's way too gun shy to let any man near her."

"Well, just as long as she keeps sending food like this, I'm okay with the whole situation."

But, Virgil wasn't. He wanted more. So much more. Probably more than she was willing to give now. Maybe ever give.

He enjoyed the coffee and cinnamon roll then headed uptown. He stopped by the dry cleaners to pick up his laundry and to drop off the basket. He didn't say anything because he didn't think she wanted the women she worked with to know, but he mouthed a thank you.

Then he went to the bank. He walked in and noticed Briggs waiting on several customers. Mr. Stewart stepped out from behind his desk and came over. "Good morning, Sheriff. As you can see, Mr. Cox has accepted my offer and he was able to start right away."

"I'm glad to see it."

"In between customers he and I have been trying to come up with some ideas for other employees. I'm confident we'll make it all work."

"I am too. I'll be on my way. I just wanted to check and see how it went."

"Very pleased to see you again, Sheriff. If you see Mr. Clevenger, tell him I send my thanks."

"I'll let Miss Cora do that. Getting Briggs, I mean, Mr. Cox, this job was her idea."

"Doesn't she work at the cleaners?"

"Yes."

"Very nice young lady."

Virgil didn't know how he'd feel if he knew the truth about Cora and he was hoping the president wouldn't suggest offering Cora a job.

Looking at Briggs smiling, Virgil got an idea. He jumped back in his black and white and headed north. He pulled to a stop in front of his parent's home.

His mother was out watering her fall flowers. She put her hand above her eyes shielding her face from the sun. "What're you doing out this way?"

"Decided I'd come by and see how it's going."

"We're fine. You don't have to worry."

"I'm not worried, I just wanted to say hello. I know you can walk to the store, I know you can care for yourself, so I'm just being neighborly."

He walked past his mother and into the house. His father stood at the kitchen sink rinsing out his coffee cup. "Morning, dad."

"Howdy. What you doin' out here?"

"Came to ask you what you're going to do with the old station in town."

"Huh?"

"Well, you just sort of closed down the filling station and called it quits. You have any intentions of selling it or you going to just keep paying taxes on it?"

"I never gave it any thought."

"Well, maybe it's time you do."

His father's face turned sour. "Nobody's going to buy that place. Not after *Eddie and Sons* opened that fancy place right across the street."

"It's just a gas station."

"Aw, he sells snacks, soda pop, tires, hell you can practically do your grocery shopping there."

Virgil shrugged. "You could sell all that stuff, too."

"I'm not competing with anyone. People want to go there they can."

"You had a good business that took care of your family for years. People came from miles around to your station. Then someone moves across the street and you close up shop."

"I didn't want the damn competition, I said."

"Why?"

"If he took only half the business I had, there wouldn't be enough for us to keep the place going."

"Yes, there would. You wouldn't be rich, but you'd still make a good living."

"I don't want to work no more."

"Why not. You're still young."

Anger flashed in his father's eyes. "I'm not that damn young."

"You're not that damn old either."

Roy Carter slapped the countertop and glared. "What are you getting at, son?"

He hadn't called Virgil that in a long time. It brought back a flood of memories and they were all good. Virgil turned away to bat the tears from his eyes.

His mother came in from outside and went to the kitchen. "You want some coffee?"

"No, I just dropped by to talk to dad."

"What about?"

His father threw down the teacup towel. "He's talking nonsense about the old station."

"Your dad's too old for that."

Virgil balled his fists. "You two never cease to amaze me. You're so damn scared you don't know how to live anymore."

His mother pointed her finger and narrowed her eyes. A look he'd grown up with and knew meant business came across her face. "Now you listen to me. Don't you come around here telling us what to do. We're not so damn old we can't make our own decisions."

"Decisions like it's safer to not love your son so that if he dies it won't hurt so much. Decisions that if you cut ties to your friends when they die it won't be such a loss. And decisions to close a successful business because that put you smack dab in the middle of a community you care about."

"That's a bunch of malarkey."

"The hell it is. You're surrounded by fear. You two are so afraid of living you don't know how anymore." Virgil turned and walked out the door. His mother called his name but he got in his automobile and drove away. He was sick of trying. Sick of hoping they'd wake up someday and decide to live again and forget the past.

Not forget they lost two sons, but remember they still had one. He fought back tears all the way to town. He found himself parked in front of the dry cleaners. He looked out as Cora waited on a customer. Smiling and carrying on with her life.

She'd faced the toughest odds and yet she smiled. Why couldn't others?

CHAPTER FIFTEEN

Cora met the boys at school and Jack had finally been given a report card. He and Ronnie were excited to show her. She buttoned a coat she'd given to Ronnie. The owner had left town without picking it up from the dry cleaners over a year ago.

No one knew how to find who it belonged to, but the coat fit Ronnie perfectly. Looking at the report cards, Cora was pleased that Jack had been a good student and got high marks in citizenship. Ronnie, on the other hand, had difficulties reading and suffered from poor health habits. And he also needed help with spelling.

She wondered how pleased Warren would be to see the low marks. Perhaps, if Ronnie were lucky, he wouldn't even notice. Maybe she could take the report card over and help explain how she could help Ronnie.

"Ronnie, you haven't been bringing your spelling words home to practice. Why not?"

He shrugged. "I guess I don't care. My pa never helped me before and now the words are too hard."

"You start bringing your spelling words home and we'll practice. Also, what's this about not having good health habits?"

Jack spoke up. "That means you use your napkin, wash your hands and don't sneeze on people."

"Ronnie, why haven't you been doing that?"

Ronnie shrugged. "I don't know. I guess because no one told me."

"The teacher did."

"Yeah, but sometimes I forget."

She stopped and leaned down and looked into Ronnie's brown eyes. "From here on out, young man, you will practice health habits, you will learn to read and know your spelling words." She reached out to touch his cheek and he flinched. She caressed his face then kissed him gently on the forehead. "You're a bright boy, Ronnie and I know you can do better. Do we understand each other?"

"Yes, ma'am."

"Good, let's get home. The weather's turning nasty."

After they entered the house and hung up their coats, Maggie ran into the house. "I'm so excited. Briggs got the job."

"That's wonderful."

"He was so excited at lunch. He just grabbed a sandwich then ran back to work. He really likes working for Harry."

"That makes me so happy. You must thank Earl. He's the one who did the talking."

"I can't imagine why the bank president would pay an ounce of attention to him, but I did go over there and told him we really appreciated his help. Of course, he denied everything."

They laughed. "That's his personality."

"The foreman at the mine was very understanding. He knew Briggs wasn't cut out to do manual labor. He's nearly as excited as we are."

"Working for the bank isn't just a job, it's a career."

"One he can do without enduring so much pain."

"We all need to be so thankful."

"Are you going to Helen's daughter's wedding Saturday."

"Yes, she invited me and the boys. I'm looking forward to it." Cora glanced outside. "I only hope the weather holds."

"Well, it's inside the church, so we'll all survive." Maggie walked to the door. "I have to get home and start dinner. I'll talk to you later." With a wave, she was out the door.

Cora went to the kitchen and saw a bushel basket full of apples, a smaller basket of pears and a sack of pecans. She looked at her neighbor's house and smiled. She put the goodies under the shelves and began cooking dinner. She'd make sure Earl would enjoy a nice dessert tonight.

She thought about Virgil almost kissing her last night and her discomfort grew. She didn't want to get into a relationship with anyone. She wasn't worthy of love. Of a normal life, a family.

No.

Too much had happened in that dark, dreary place where they held her captive for five years. Day after day of abuse, neglect, and torment. That was all there was to look forward to. She often wondered if her father realized the life he'd sentenced his daughter to in order to keep his stellar name and remain in good graces with the right people.

She wanted to hate him. She wanted to strike him, and make him pay for all that'd happened to her, but she refused to allow him to control her. No more. In spite of everything, she'd come out alive, gotten a job, had Jack and smiled every single day.

She knew her father didn't because happiness couldn't get past the blackness in his heart. There was no room for love, tenderness, or kindness.

They sat down to dinner and after the dishes were done and she'd helped Ronnie with reading and spelling, she put the boys to bed and took out some mending to do.

Two apple and pear cobblers sat cooling on the counter. She planned to drop off Earl's when Maggie walked the boys to school. A knock sounded at the door and Cora suspected Virgil Carter waited on the other side.

She answered and her suspicions were true. However, he stood with two ice cold sodas in his outstretched hand. "I come bringing gifts and I'm not hungry."

She smiled. Taking the drinks she walked into the kitchen for an opener. Flipping off the caps she handed him one and they toasted. "To good friends."

His smile slipped. "To more than friendship."

She took a drink, not taking her eyes off him. It fizzed all the way down her throat and made her eyes water. "Those are so good, but the first swallow always burns a little."

"I only plan to stay a few minutes. I know you have things to do. I wanted to tell you that I hadn't forgotten I'd paint your house, lay the flooring and do a few minor repairs."

"Need I remind you that you don't have to do that?"

"We reached an agreement and I'm a man of my word."

She took another swallow. "I know your job keeps you very busy."

"I don't have a thing to do when I'm not working. I'll start this Saturday. Then I'm taking everyone to dinner."

"That isn't necessary."

"No, it isn't, but it'll be fun."

"You'll spoil us. Tonight soda pop." She looked at him. "What's next?"

"Maybe a little surprise."

"I'm excited for Briggs."

"I am too. I went to the bank today and he was busy waiting on customers. I hope it works out for him."

He pointed to the stove. "What that?"

"Cobbler. Would you like a piece?"

"No, I told myself I wasn't going to eat your food. You're a single mother working to put food on the table and here I come along and eat it all."

"Well, a little cobbler won't be missed."

"It does smell delicious."

"Come on and I'll dish you up a bowl."

"I assume the other one's for Earl?"

"I wanted to thank him for mentioning Briggs to the bank president." She wrinkled her brow as she reached for a spoon. "However, I don't know what kind of influence he has over Mr. Stewart."

"I don't either."

"I know so little about his life. What did he do?"

"He was once mayor of the town and very well liked. He helped a lot of needy people. Even when the vets came back from the war, he was right there on Main Street shaking military personnel hands. Helping them find jobs, a place to stay, a hot meal."

They sat at the table. "Maggie came by earlier and she's walking on a cloud. She's so happy. They weren't sure how much longer Briggs could continue to do all the physical labor in the mines."

"I know. And it was a waste because Briggs is a smart man. Knows his numbers and he's done a great job with the town budget."

"Speaking of money, did you hear any more about Bart?"

"I spoke to Gene briefly but he didn't have much to add to the case. Harriet is talking, but Bart's as tight-lipped as ever."

"Jack and Ronnie received their first report cards."

"Oh, how'd they do?"

"Jack did very well. But Ronnie is struggling in a few areas. I've started working with him on his reading and spelling."

"Did Warren see it yet?"

"No, I've been afraid to take it over there." She put her spoon down. "You never know when he's going to fly off the handle and beat the child."

"That's for sure. I'd hold off as long as I could if I were you."

"I'm very tempted to sign the card myself. But, I know that would be wrong and I'd be embarrassed if Miss Potter found out."

"She's aware of what goes on in that house."

She bit her lip. "I wonder if you might talk to the principal. See if there is some way around Warren having to sign the report."

"I can try, but the school has certain rules they won't break regardless of the situation."

She let out a breath. "I guess you're right. I'll take it to him tomorrow."

"Are you going to Sam and Martha's wedding this Saturday?"

"Yes, I thought I'd bring the boys."

Virgil took a sip of coffee. "I'll be glad to come by and walk with you."

"I think that would be great. I'm excited. Helen is a nervous wreck. I think we're going to tell her to take tomorrow off, and then we're closing the dry cleaners Saturday."

"That's a good idea. She probably has a lot of things to do."

"We've all been helping in our spare time, but there's nothing like a full day to get ready for a wedding."

"I'm glad for the couple. They've been dating for well over a year."

"That's what Helen said."

"Well, I need to get going so you can get ready for bed." She stood. "Thanks for coming by."

"You know, I'm here most evenings."

"I know, and I enjoy your company."

"Nothing else?"

"Virgil, there is a lot in my past that you don't want to know about."

"That's where you're wrong. I do want to know. Simply so we can put it out of the way."

She shook her head. "It's far from simple."

He took her by the arms and held her in front of him. "I care about you. You must know that by now."

"I can't return those feelings, Virgil. I simply can't." She pulled from his grasp. "Everything is too fresh. Too soon. Too hurtful."

CHAPTER SIXTEEN

Virgil stepped back. "I'm sorry, I won't push you. I can only imagine what you've been through. But I hope someday you can share it with me and start healing. In a way I understand how you feel. I don't like talking about the war and all the stuff that went on then."

"Let's hope we can both find healing."

"I'll wait."

With that he left because there was nothing more that he could say. He'd never felt this way before. He wanted to take her in his arms and comfort her but he knew she didn't want that.

She wanted her past all rolled up in a tight ball so nothing could touch her heart but Jack. He wanted her to know that her love would be safe in his hands, that he'd protect her, that she was all that mattered to him.

Saturday morning, he was at Cora's bright and early, planning to get started on painting the house. He knew the weather would be turning colder soon and he'd be forced inside.

After lunch, he left to get dressed for the afternoon wedding. He met Cora, who looked prettier than any bride he'd ever seen before. She had on a stunning two-piece suit with heels and a beautiful necklace.

It was obvious that, at one time, Cora had lived a life few in Gibbs City, Missouri could imagine. The boys were spotless, with shined shoes and neat jackets.

If only Ronnie's hair would settle down. Pal felt a little left out when they shut him up in the back porch, but he soon settled down.

Virgil, Cora and the boys walked to church. They met up with Maggie and Briggs on the way and talked about Briggs' new job. Cora had a gift she carried for the bride.

Inside, the church was all decorated with crepe paper and red and white flowers sat on the altar, the pews, and at the entrance of the building.

A white cloth covered the path to the front of the church, and the groom nervously joked with a couple of his friends as he waited for the bride.

Virgil sat beside Cora and slipped his arm around the back of the seat. She gave him a weary looked and he smiled. The boys were excited because this was their first wedding and the excitement of having no idea what was going to happen had them both struggling to stay seated.

Soon the organist played "*Here Comes the Bride*" and everyone stood. Helen's daughter looked lovely in the long, white gown. Her father proudly walked the stunning young girl to meet her new husband. Sam and Martha made a stunning couple.

As they stood at the front of the church, Virgil leaned down and asked, "Does this put you in the mood for your own wedding?"

She smiled, than faked a glare. "You're incorrigible."

After the "*I do's*" and the congratulations, they gathered for a reception at a local hall. A young woman stood at the microphone in front of a small band. Virgil took Cora by the arm and led her to the dance floor. If she planned to refuse, she'd have to make a scene, because he was determined to have one dance.

The slow music had him pulling her close and pressing his hand into the middle of her back. She fit into his arms perfectly. As they moved across the floor and swayed to the music, he pressed his cheek against her and inhaled her perfume.

She relaxed a little and soon they were the only two people in the world on a stage as wide as the sky. The scent of her, the feel of her and the presence of her boggled his mind and sped up his heart.

He wanted this woman like nothing in his life.

All too soon the music stopped and they broke apart.

After the wedding they went to Betty's Diner for dinner. The boys chattered about the cake and laughed about everyone throwing rice at the couple as they left. They only stopped long enough to devour hamburgers and fries and a coke. She ordered meatloaf and Virgil had roast beef. The boys were anxious to move. They'd sat too long in the church and had energy to burn.

They slowly walked home and Virgil was so glad he had this time with Cora, Jack and Ronnie. It was almost as if they were a family, just the four of them.

Then something struck his mind that never had before. Other children. Did he want more children? If he married today would he want a big family or maybe one child or two? He'd never gotten that far in his thoughts of settling down.

But he liked the size they were right now. He looked down at Cora. "It might rain tomorrow. If it does, I'll put the flooring down."

"It's Sunday, you should be in church."

He smiled. "I might join you there. I usually don't go because Sunday is a day I catch up on all the paperwork of the week. I'm going to start leaving that to John. Give him a little more responsibility."

"Good, we'll look for you at church tomorrow."

They stood outside her house. When she didn't invite him in, disappointment settled in his chest. They'd spent most of the day together so he didn't mind so much. He planned to make up for it tomorrow.

The next day, icy hail pelted the whole city and Virgil was barely able to make it to Cora's house on the slick roads. Inside, the smell of pancakes filled the little house. "I think church has been canceled. Nobody's moving around out there."

He took off his oil slicker and hung it on a nearby hook. She offered him a cup of coffee. "The boys are going to be bored to death today."

"No place to spend all that energy."

"You want some pancakes? I made extra batter."

"Don't mind if I do."

"Thank you for dinner last night. The food wasn't that great, but it's always good to eat something I didn't cook."

"Betty's food is barely edible. But no one complains because she has the only diner in town."

"Well, it was a wonderful gesture on your part. The boys talked about it all night."

The sizzle of the skillet, the boys laughing in the bedroom about something and Pal lying quietly next to his chair felt wonderful to him. More and more he looked at this as his family, when in reality he knew it wasn't.

Cora set a stack of four pancakes and five strips of bacon on a plate in front of him. He picked up his fork and began eating.

"I don't know if it's a good idea today to work on the kitchen floor with the boys running through the house. It might be better if you fixed the sink in the bathroom."

"I can do that."

"I feel bad with you doing all this for us. I can only imagine what the townspeople are saying about the two of us."

"Don't let that bother you."

"Of course it bothers me. I don't want them teasing Jack and Ronnie by accusing me of being a loose woman. Someone who entertains men."

"It's only one man, and as I've said before. We're adults. What we do is none of their business."

"You know that's not how it works in a small town like Gibbs City."

"I haven't heard a word. Don't look for trouble, it'll find us."

He finished breakfast and the boys came out and visited for a while. They had him listen to their favorite cowboy show on the radio with them. Ronnie on his lap, Jack snuggled up close.

Virgil put his arm around Jack and tucked the little boy against his side. His warm body made Virgil sleepy. He'd not slept well last night, and while there were no nightmares, he couldn't get the whole wedding, family and marriage out of his mind.

He turned to look at Cora. She stood in the kitchen putting a couple of pies into the oven and straightening the kitchen as she went along. Her movements were minimal and calm, as if being in the kitchen was her favorite place to be.

He smiled. This to him was heaven. Sunday morning, his belly full, the boys hugging him and Cora cooking something special for dessert. Any man in this situation would be one helluva lucky guy.

But it wasn't him. Cora couldn't open up enough to trust him with her heart. She'd been through hell and she wasn't taking any chances. That made him determined to learn all he could about her.

He didn't want to pry, but if he was going to fight a demon, he had to know what the monster looked like.

Just as the boys' program ended, Maggie came over. "Can Jack and Ronnie come and play with Tommy?"

"Oh my goodness," Cora said. "You must be insane."

"No, Briggs is allowing them to put up a pretend fort in the back porch out of the rain and Tommy wanted his friends to join him."

Jack and Ronnie were already looking for their shoes and coats, and dashing across the street before Cora could say anything.

"Well, I guess the answer is yes, they can play at your house."

Maggie looked at Virgil. "You seem mighty comfortable sitting there like you own the place."

He laughed and stood. "Since the boys are gone, I can do what I came to do. I'm putting down the new floor covering we bought for the kitchen last weekend."

"Good luck with that."

Maggie left and he took the proper measurements and they moved out what furniture they could to clear the floor. Even the cabinets had to go.

Virgil looked at the empty kitchen. "I wish we'd replaced that stove while we were in Joplin. That thing barely works."

"I know and it's so old. I have to wait a few more months."

"Why?"

"I have to save up the money."

"Cora, I could buy you a stove."

"I didn't like you paying for what you did. I won't have you furnishing my whole house."

"Why not? I'm here all the time."

"Maybe we should change that. You're here looking for something I'm not willing to share."

He put his hands on his hips. "You don't have any idea what I want."

"Yes I do. You want to sleep with me."

He took her in his arms and pulled her reluctantly to his chest. "I want so much more than that. I'd be lying if I said I didn't want to lay with you, but I want your heart, Cora, then I'll work on your body."

He kissed the top of her head and went back to measuring. He knew she needed time to take it all in. Maybe she'd cast him aside, but he was determined not to go easily. She was his woman, and by God, he'd fight heaven and earth to have her.

CHAPTER SEVENTEEN

Cora didn't like the way Virgil talked. He was being too possessive and it scared her. He had no idea how much her past could hurt him. Tear his insides up and leave him an empty shell.

It had done that to her.

She watched as he worked, moving carefully around the kitchen. As soon as her pies were done, she removed them from the oven and set them to cool on a rack on the table.

"Call me if you need anything," she announced on the way to the bedroom. "I'll be changing sheets."

She went about her business and straightened the boys' room. Jack and Ronnie now shared the rollaway bed, but she'd need to replace it soon. They were growing so fast.

Stripping off the sheets, she planned to take them to work tomorrow and wash them there. Nothing would dry in this rain. At least the new dryers were helpful. They were far from being as useful as promised, but they helped on rainy days.

With the bedrooms cleaned, she moved to the living room. She stopped and looked at the new floor. The print design they'd picked out really brightened the room, even on a dreary day like today. It made such a difference.

As Virgil went around tapping down the edges with molding, she marveled that he'd managed to get the edge beneath the heavy stove.

"I love this."

On his hands and knees, Virgil straightened his back and looked across the floor. "It's really nice compared to the old one. It was so old I had to take it up in strips."

"I can imagine."

"It'll be all done as soon as I finished the trim."

Within a few minutes they were moving back the cabinets and the table with the chairs. She smiled. "The place looks brand new."

"It sure brightens things up."

She tapped her bottom lip and the toe of her right foot. "It makes me want to paint the walls."

He rolled his eyes and groaned. "Now you've started with the home remodeling mood?"

"I guess so."

She put on a pot of coffee and after Virgil washed up, they relaxed at the kitchen table. "I never realized you were so handy."

"I'd meant to do this sooner but hadn't gotten around to it." He took the cup she offered. "If we run into a problem, I can contact Ethan Mercer. I don't think you've met him, but he's kind of the jack-of-all-trades around town."

"The name doesn't sound familiar."

"He's a young veteran with three young children. While he was off fighting the war, his wife Veronica took off to Las Vegas with a traveling salesman."

Cora inhaled sharply. "She left her children?"

Virgil nodded. "Sent him divorce papers while he was fighting in Europe."

"How on earth does he manage?"

"His mother, Norma, cares for the children, but she's having some health issues."

"What are the ages of the children? Perhaps I can have them over to play with Jack."

Virgil cocked his head. "I don't know for sure. It seems like Frank is seven or eight, and the other boy, Willis, must be five or six. Then there's Lizzy. She's only three."

"He must've come home during the war."

Virgil looked away. "Veronica claims she went to California to meet Ethan on leave once and conceived Lizzy during that time."

"But, you don't believe that?"

"I believe what Ethan says. He's a decent, honest man and he says Lizzy is his."

"Then that's the end of it. I'll ask Miss Potter to point out the children when I fetch the boys from school tomorrow."

Virgil stood. "I have to run out and check on my folks. Would you and the boys like to come?"

"No, I'm going to get them back home and help Ronnie with his studies."

She walked him to the door and watched as he dashed through the sleet to his car. He'd been a great help today, but it still made her nervous being around him sometimes.

She remembered being arrested. Three policemen came to her door that day. They threw her against the wall and handcuffed her without saying a word. The bigger one with the bad breath kept his forearm across the back of her neck, making it impossible for her to move.

Without a warrant or any authority they went through her house. Then one on each side, they dragged her to the parked police car even though she was perfectly capable of walking. At the station, they threw her in a cell without food, water or a toilet for twenty-one hours. During that time, they never told her what she was being charged with.

No, her memory of the police and their authority still haunted her nights.

She'd barely made it back to the kitchen when someone pounded on her door. Thinking Virgil had forgotten something, she ran and flung the door wide. Head prison guard Herbert Grubber stood on the small back porch.

Her heart pounded so loud she was certain he could hear it. Her hand instinctively rose to her throat. "What do you want?"

He had a hooded slicker on that covered most of his face. "Warden Becker wanted me to come down here and see how you were doing."

"Get out of here and leave me alone. You've got no right to harass me." She gritted her teeth. "I'm a free woman, Mr. Grubber. If you so much as look at me the wrong way, my attorney wants to hear about it."

"If you know what's good for you, you won't be so smart. And stop hanging around with that sheriff."

"Or what?"

"Something just might happen to that little kid you got living with you."

"If you dare..."

"Yeah, yeah, yeah. Shut your damn trap and do what you're told." A malicious grin curled his lips. "Like I taught you." He clipped her under the chin. "Remember?"

He turned, got in his car and drove away. Her hands trembled. Fear as cold as ice and painful as fire poured over her body. She slumped against the wall and slowly slid to the floor.

Tears filled her eyes and soon she sobbed hysterically. If anything happened to Jack, she'd die. What was she to do? Her first thought was to run as far away as possible. To hide where no one could find them. Christ Almighty, they'd been watching her all this time.

CHAPTER EIGHTEEN

Virgil wanted to check the office before going to visit his folks to see that they were all right. They still preferred a wood burning stove and he didn't want his father hauling wood into the house.

The station was quiet. John hadn't left any messages. Virgil went to Frank's and made sure it'd been all quiet around the station.

He and Frank sat inside the firehouse and watched the sleet that had turned to rain. "The judge said he was going to see about getting you some extra help at the next council meeting."

"We'll see. I technically work for the county, and if the town hired anyone they'd be under the council instead of me. Room for lots of conflict."

"I didn't think about that. I guess that could be more of a curse than any help."

"I'll see if the judge won't consider talking to the county commissioner and see how he feels about an additional person. Even if we just had a jailer. That would free me and John up for other things."

"And a jailer doesn't have to be a licensed Police Officer."

"No, they do require some training, but not as much as John and I had."

"Well, that sounds like the way to go. The county is always going to be looking for ways to save money."

"People like living in towns and counties with lots of benefits, but no one wants to pay taxes."

"Nothing we can do about that." Frank put his booted foot on the fender of the fire truck. "What'd you think of that wedding yesterday? Kind of nice wasn't it?"

"Very nice. Briggs said they were driving to Kansas City for a honeymoon."

Frank chuckled. "Me and Mae were sitting behind you and Cora wondering if you two might not be next."

Virgil smiled at the thought. "If I had my way I'd marry her today. But, she's leery because of all the horrible things that happened in prison."

"Virgil, those places leave grown men with horrible scars, imagine what it does to a woman."

"I know, and trust me, I'm trying to be patient."

"That's the smart thing to do. Women are strange creatures. I been married twenty years and Mae manages to surprise me all the time."

"Did I hear my name?" Mae came out with a tray of sandwiches and coffee. She set it on the table. "Here's some lunch. Only two crazy men would sit out here in the cold and watch it rain."

"We're talking."

"You're crazy. It's winter, for crying out loud." She shivered and went back inside.

Frank took a half a sandwich. "See, what I was saying? Who thinks it's winter in October?"

Virgil moved around and stomped his feet before taking a sip of coffee. "I think the weather is just fine."

After they had lunch, Virgil stuck his head in and thanked Mae before he left to visit his parents. He drove by Cora's on the way out of town and saw a man getting into a car. Virgil didn't recognize him, but he gave him a hard stare.

Virgil turned around and followed the car until it crossed the county line then he pulled over. He wrote down the license

CHAPTER EIGHTEEN

Virgil wanted to check the office before going to visit his folks to see that they were all right. They still preferred a wood burning stove and he didn't want his father hauling wood into the house.

The station was quiet. John hadn't left any messages. Virgil went to Frank's and made sure it'd been all quiet around the station.

He and Frank sat inside the firehouse and watched the sleet that had turned to rain. "The judge said he was going to see about getting you some extra help at the next council meeting."

"We'll see. I technically work for the county, and if the town hired anyone they'd be under the council instead of me. Room for lots of conflict."

"I didn't think about that. I guess that could be more of a curse than any help."

"I'll see if the judge won't consider talking to the county commissioner and see how he feels about an additional person. Even if we just had a jailer. That would free me and John up for other things."

"And a jailer doesn't have to be a licensed Police Officer."

"No, they do require some training, but not as much as John and I had."

"Well, that sounds like the way to go. The county is always going to be looking for ways to save money."

"People like living in towns and counties with lots of benefits, but no one wants to pay taxes."

"Nothing we can do about that." Frank put his booted foot on the fender of the fire truck. "What'd you think of that wedding yesterday? Kind of nice wasn't it?"

"Very nice. Briggs said they were driving to Kansas City for a honeymoon."

Frank chuckled. "Me and Mae were sitting behind you and Cora wondering if you two might not be next."

Virgil smiled at the thought. "If I had my way I'd marry her today. But, she's leery because of all the horrible things that happened in prison."

"Virgil, those places leave grown men with horrible scars, imagine what it does to a woman."

"I know, and trust me, I'm trying to be patient."

"That's the smart thing to do. Women are strange creatures. I been married twenty years and Mae manages to surprise me all the time."

"Did I hear my name?" Mae came out with a tray of sandwiches and coffee. She set it on the table. "Here's some lunch. Only two crazy men would sit out here in the cold and watch it rain."

"We're talking."

"You're crazy. It's winter, for crying out loud." She shivered and went back inside.

Frank took a half a sandwich. "See, what I was saying? Who thinks it's winter in October?"

Virgil moved around and stomped his feet before taking a sip of coffee. "I think the weather is just fine."

After they had lunch, Virgil stuck his head in and thanked Mae before he left to visit his parents. He drove by Cora's on the way out of town and saw a man getting into a car. Virgil didn't recognize him, but he gave him a hard stare.

Virgil turned around and followed the car until it crossed the county line then he pulled over. He wrote down the license plate number so he could find out who'd been visiting Cora. Not because he was jealous, but because the look on the man's face didn't appear all that friendly.

He rode out to his parent's house and loaded up his arms with a pile of wood before going inside. "I'll fill up the firewood box while I'm here."

His father stood. "I was just going to go around and get the wheelbarrow and fetch more wood."

"Now you don't have to."

After four trips outside, the box was full and would last his folks several days. His mother pulled out a kitchen chair. "I made some bean soup if you're hungry."

He wasn't, but he didn't want to seem rude. He sat at the same table he'd been raised at, in the same chair and ate his supper in silence. He remembered a time when you couldn't get a word in edgewise with all the chatter.

Now, the silence was sad and chilling. There wasn't his oldest brother, James, teasing Sam, the youngest, about what a pipsqueak he was. Nor was his mother complaining how the three boys were growing out of their clothes before she could buy them and get them home from the store.

James wasn't talking about his sweetheart at the time and Sam wasn't there talking about becoming a teacher someday. The war had robbed them of all that. Snuffed out their lives without leaving anything to fill the void. Just heartache and tears.

His dad leaned back and said, "Winter is coming. I don't think it will be early or worse than last year, but there'll be more snow for sure."

"According to the Farmer's Almanac this is going to be a bad year."

"Well, I hope it's wrong. We don't need all that snow. People can't get out of their houses and the roads are a mess."

"I'm glad we have plenty of firewood. I remember last year you were chopping wood before Christmas."

His dad shook his head. "I don't want that this year."

Virgil finished his soup and leaned back in his chair. "I didn't see you two at the wedding yesterday."

His mother rubbed her back. "I didn't feel like getting out."

"I could've picked you up."

"Saw Doris this morning and she said you were there with that prison woman and those two brats."

Virgil paused and took a deep, calming breath before he could speak. His chest constricted. "That's Miss Cora Williams and the 'brats' are her parentless nephew and little Ronnie Hayes who gets beaten regularly. She takes him every chance she can to protect him."

"She's an ex-con isn't she?"

"Yes, she was in prison."

"That what you were raised to go after? A woman that's done more than any decent lady would imagine?"

Virgil didn't say anything. He respected his mother too much. He thanked her for the meal, put his hat on, slipped on his coat and walked out the door.

If his mother was thinking like that, what were the other people imagining? Did Cora even stand a chance here? What if she'd taken him up on his offer to drive with him to his parents' home? Would his mother slam the door in her face?

This was never going to work. There was such a gap between him and his parents that he now knew would never be bridged. He'd never bring Cora home to meet his family and eventually she'd find out why.

CHAPTER NINETEEN

After Grubber left, Cora pulled herself together before Jack came in, soaking wet. She quickly removed his coat and put him by the heater. "Where is Ronnie?"

"His dad came and got him."

Cora's heart fluttered. "Why did he do that?"

Jack shrugged. "He said he saw Miss Potter last night when she was leaving the wedding and she said something to him about Ronnie not doing his school work."

"Stay here. I'm going to see if I can get Ronnie."

She only had the coat over her shoulder when she ran to Ronnie's house. She knocked on the door. Cold wind chilled her all the way through her clothes, but she was more worried about Ronnie.

She knocked again. "Mr. Hayes, are you there?"

Where else would they be?

She pounded frantically. "Open the door. Ronnie, are you in there?"

She saw Virgil's squad car driving down the street and she waved her arms. Drenched, she ran toward him. "Warren went to Maggie's and took Ronnie. I can't get him to open the door."

Virgil grabbed his coat getting out of the vehicle. She touched his arm. "Should we wait a few minutes and see if Ronnie shows up."

"What if he doesn't?"

"Then you need to get in there."

Virgil slipped his arms in the coat and opened the back door. "You wait in the car."

Virgil dashed up the stairs and jumped onto Warren's porch. He knocked so loudly she feared the whole neighborhood heard. He waited a few minutes and still no one answered. Soon, Virgil was pounding on the door with his fists.

"Warren, I know you're in there. Open the door. I just want to check on Ronnie."

Still no answer. Virgil waited, she waited, the rain pelting the car windows. The cold settled across her shoulders and fear crept up her spine. She glanced to her left and saw Maggie hugging herself as she waited on her porch. Soon a loud crash sounded as Virgil kicked down the door and disappeared inside.

Loud shouting and screams and slamming of furniture had every neighbor looking at Warren's house. Cora fell out of the car and ran toward the house just as Virgil came out, Ronnie lying limp in his arms.

"Is he alive?"

"I don't know. Let's get him to the hospital."

She took off her coat and wrapped it around Ronnie's battered body. His tiny face so swollen she barely recognized him.

Inside the car, she rolled the window down. "Maggie, Ronnie's hurt, we're going to the hospital. Will you look after Jack?"

Briggs was already putting his coat on. "Let us know."

Virgil hit the siren and they headed for the hospital. She touched his throat and felt a weak pulse. "He's alive."

"We're only a few minutes away."

"I don't want to move him because I'm not sure if anything is broken."

"I found him on the kitchen floor in a pool of dried blood."

"Where was his father?"

"Passed out on the couch. An empty bottle in one hand, a strap in the other."

"What kind of strap?" She shoved his hair back. "He's too little to take this kind of beating and survive."

"Let's hope we got to him in time."

They hit the emergency entrance and Virgil ran around the car and cradled Ronnie in his arms. They crashed through the doors of the hospital. "We have a wounded child here," Virgil shouted. "We need a doctor immediately."

A nurse came from behind her desk. "Bring him in here." She turned to another nurse. "Quick, go get Dr. Lowery."

Ronnie looked so helpless and small. Cora couldn't keep the tears at bay. Gently, with the help of the nurse, they removed the coat and Cora's knees nearly buckled.

As the nurse cut off Ronnie's blood-soaked clothing, Virgil gripped her shoulder. "He'll get the care he needs now."

"But can they save him?"

Ronnie's face had been beaten severely and both eyes were swollen shut, his lips were so swollen they'd turned blood red. A long gash at the corner of his left eye would need stitches to close.

Ronnie moaned. Cora took his hand. "It's Aunt Cora, Ronnie. The sheriff and I are here for you."

"Pa?"

Virgil leaned down and put his lips close to Ronnie's ear. "He'll never hurt you again, son. Not ever."

Dr. Lowery came in and shook hands with the sheriff. "This doesn't surprise me, Virgil."

"Me either. Miss Williams has been keeping the boy to protect him from Warren, but he got to him today."

"I bet he was drinking."

"Drunk as a skunk. Passed out and I doubt he'll even remember this."

The doctor slowly undressed Ronnie and made sure no bones were broken. He then turned him over and Ronnie's back was torn up with cuts, welts and covered with blood. Cora gasped in horror.

Virgil put his arms around her and walked her to the waiting room. The nurse brought in a glass of water and squeezed her arm. Her hands shook too much to take the water. She buried her face in Virgil's coat front and cried.

He rubbed her back and spoke soft words, but nothing could take the brutal images from her mind. She couldn't understand how a parent could be so inhumane.

She cried until she couldn't cry any more.

Soon the doctor came to speak to them. They both stood up. Virgil clutched her hand. "He's beaten very badly. I've given him something for the pain. Nothing is broken, but it will take weeks for him to heal."

"What about the deep cuts?"

"There were four places we stitched up. The one by his eye is the most serious."

Virgil squeezed her hand. "Can we take him home?"

"The law says I can only release a child to his parent."

"Well, then I'll take him and you can file charges against me."

"I'm not going to do that, Virgil. Take the boy. But, you're going to have to deal with his father."

"I plan to deal with him, all right."

They went into the room where Ronnie sat wrapped in a sheet. Virgil gently touched his shoulder. "You ready to go home?"

"No."

"How about Aunt Cora's."

He nodded.

While Virgil carried Ronnie to the car, Cora took the pain medication from the doctor, along with instructions on Ronnie's care. Dr. Lowery wanted to see him in two days.

She sat in the car and Virgil gently placed him on her lap and quickly covered them with his coat. Ronnie was out before Virgil reached the other side of the car.

CHAPTER TWENTY

Virgil was so angry he could hardly drive. After seeing what Warren had done to tiny, little Ronnie, he knew he could choke the man to death with his bare hands. He had to get control of his anger before he did something crazy.

He managed to get Cora and Ronnie into the house. Cora dressed the boy in his pajamas and got a little soup down his throat before he collapsed onto Jack's bed.

While she put together sandwiches, Virgil went across the street. Cora wanted Ronnie in bed before Jack saw him for fear his appearance would frighten the child.

Maggie met him at the door. "How is he?"

"Bad."

"Oh my God. That man is a monster."

"Nothing was broken, but he took a strap to his back and it looks like he used his face as a punching bag."

Maggie shook her head in disbelief. "How can he do that?"

"I don't know, but I plan to deal with him."

Maggie took Virgil by the arm. "Let it sit for a few days. Don't go over there tonight. He's too drunk and you're too mad."

Virgil looked at Warren's house. "I'd like to do to him what he did to Ronnie."

"I know. It's all I can do to keep Briggs from going over there and blowing his head off. But let it go and care for Ronnie. There will be time to deal with his dad."

"Don't call that man a dad. He's nothing but a rotten son of a bitch that deserves to die."

"I know, but right now, Ronnie needs all of us if he's going to heal."

"I know. Is Jack ready to go home?"

"Come on in." Jack and Tommy laid on the floor while Maggie's middle boy read a book to them. "Jack, it's time to go home."

"Hi, Virgil." He ran for his coat.

Maggie came forward with a dish in her outstretched hands. "I made a casserole because I knew Cora would be too upset."

"Thanks for your help, Maggie. We both really appreciate all you and Briggs have done."

"She's done much more for us. Plus, Ronnie needs her."

Virgil and Jack ran across the street and Virgil put the casserole on the table and removed Jack's coat.

Jack looked around. "Where's Ronnie."

Cora put her arm around Jack and led him into the bedroom. "Jack, Ronnie's father is very bad. He punished Ronnie too harshly and Ronnie had to go to the hospital. He's going to be okay, but he has to heal. He's very sore and in a lot of pain."

Jack walked over and bent down then he looked at Cora. "Is that Ronnie?"

"Yes, it is sweetheart."

Jack tiptoed back to where they stood. He put his hand next to his mouth and whispered, "I'll be real quiet."

"That's good. Tonight, I think it best if you sleep in bed with me. This way you won't accidently bump into him and wake him up."

"Okay. But where's the sheriff going to sleep?"

Cora looked at Virgil. "He'll go home tonight and sleep there."

"But what if Mr. Hayes comes to get Ronnie?" Tears filled Jack's eyes. "What if he hurts you or me?"

Cora pressed him to her chest. "He won't. We'll lock the door and we'll be safe."

He clutched Cora's shoulders. "But, what if he breaks in? What if he has a gun? Aunt Cora, I'm really scared."

Virgil patted him on the back. "Okay buddy, I'll sleep here on the couch until this is settled."

Jack calmed down immediately and Cora sat him at the table with a plate of Maggie's ham and potato casserole and a glass of milk.

Cora pulled Virgil into the living room. "I'm not sure you spending the night is a good idea."

"I'm sure it isn't, but think about Jack. He's scared to death Warren is going to come over here and hurt someone."

"I know but people will talk."

"Right now, I couldn't care less. I almost dare someone to say something to me."

Her eyes saddened. "They won't say anything to you, Virgil, it will be me or Jack they attack."

He took her by the arm. "I can't help it, Cora. I won't leave you and Jack here alone. And Ronnie is going to need help."

She wrung her hands. "I don't know what to do."

"We could get married."

"No," she answered quickly. "I can't do that." She turned away. "I won't."

His heart ached and he felt the fool. Was he so damn desperate to have her that he'd blackmail her into marriage? Of course, she didn't want to marry him. Why would she? He didn't have anything to offer but a bunch of bad memories and a tough job that no one wanted.

"I'm sorry. I shouldn't have said that."

Her face had reddened and her hands shook. "Maybe you could stay just tonight. I mean," she rubbed her forehead. "I don't know what I mean."

She slumped on the couch. "There's so much you don't know, Virgil. So much I can't tell you."

"I understand," he managed to say. The hurt in his chest expanded to the point he couldn't remember a time he felt so helpless. Not even during the war. There he could always shoot his way out or run or throw a grenade. This was completely out of his area of expertise.

Jack finished dinner and came into the living room. Virgil bent down and looked into his blue eyes. "Hey, want to go with me to the station so I can get my stuff?"

Jack's brows pulled together. "What stuff?"

"If I'm going to spend the night, I need my shaving gear, clean clothes, and my other boots."

"Sure, can we turn on the siren?"

"No, there's been enough excitement. Let's just get to the station and back as fast as we can."

Jack looked at Cora. "She gonna be okay?"

"Yes, she'll watch Ronnie and we'll be right back."

Jack ran for his coat. "Okay."

Virgil looked at her. "Lock the door. We won't be long."

She nodded and followed them to the door and closed it behind them. He heard the lock slip into place before and he and Jack hurried to the squad car. They pulled up to the station just as the sun disappeared and street lights flickered on.

He took Jack by the hand and unlocked the station door. He quickly scribbled John a note then went into his room to gather a few things.

"Is this where you live, Virgil?"

"Yeah, this is home."

Jack looked around frowning. "I feel really bad for you. This isn't really a house."

"It's the best I have." He grabbed a leather valise and put his personal items in and folded his clothes on top.

For a moment he thought of letting Frank know what was going on, but thought differently. He didn't want to leave Cora alone any longer than necessary.

He and Jack arrived back at Cora's in time for her to have piled several blankets, a pillow and a sheet on the couch. He put his bag out of the way, so no one would trip over it then went to check on Ronnie.

Cora followed. "I'll need to wake him soon for his pain medication. I don't want him to wake up screaming. It'll upset him and Jack both."

"Not to mention you."

She tried to smile. "Yes, I don't want to see him suffer anymore." As she walked out of the room she asked, "Do you want something to eat?"

"No, thanks."

She went to the kitchen and looked out the window. "Do you think you should go over there and fix the door? I think it's going to get cold tonight."

"Let the bastard freeze."

Cora quickly turned to Jack, who'd turned on his radio program. "Don't talk like that around him."

"He didn't hear me."

"Still, let's not stoop to Warren's level. We have to be humane about this whole thing."

Virgil walked away. "I don't."

Jack had crawled up on his temporary bed and wrapped a blanket around himself. "Hey Virgil, come listen to my show with me. This guy always gets the bad guys, just like you."

"Good for him."

Jack curled up in Virgil's lap. After a few minutes he touched Virgil's face. "Are you gonna put Ronnie's dad in jail for hurting him?"

"Let's hope we can make that happen."

"Can you at least make it where Ronnie never has to go back there again?"

"Jack, I'm going to do everything in my power to protect Ronnie."

"That's cause you're one of the good guys."

"Let's hope so."

A whimpering sound came from Jack's room. Cora rushed inside. Virgil set Jack down and went to help. "He needs to drink some water, Virgil."

He ran and got a glass and returned with a towel to put beneath his chin. He gulped several swallows before his head fell back.

"Is he okay?"

"Sheriff?"

Virgil leaned down. "Yes, Ronnie."

"Pee."

"Okay, let's get a dose of pain medication down you first."

Cora quickly poured a teaspoon of liquid and put it in his mouth. He coughed a little, but swallowed a little more water.

"He needs to go to the bathroom."

"Okay, do you need me to help you?"

"No, we guys can handle this."

She leaned closer and whispered. "He's always been a little shy."

Virgil pulled back the covers and picked up Ronnie. He didn't weigh any more than a good sized watermelon. Careful not to hurt him any more than necessary, they made it into the bathroom. Virgil took off the bottom of his pajamas should there be an accident.

Ronnie managed to get the job done and Virgil redressed him. "Jack's favorite radio show is on, do you want to listen to that for a few minutes?"

Ronnie nodded. His eyes so swollen and black and blue, Virgil worried that his vision could be impaired. Virgil walked into the living room with Ronnie in his arms and sat on the couch.

Jack moved closer and took Ronnie's hand. "You're going to be better, Ronnie."

Silently the three of them sat on the couch and listened to the radio. At some point Ronnie fell asleep, but Virgil didn't want to put him back in bed. He didn't want to let him go.

When the show was over, Cora called Jack for his bath. He was never excited about that. With as little fuss as possible, he was dressed in pajamas and in Cora's bed.

In the meantime, Virgil had put Ronnie back to bed and was in the living room when a knock sounded at the door. Virgil answered and Maggie stood there looking concerned. "How is Ronnie?"

Virgil opened the door wider. "Come in. He's okay. The medicine keeps him sleeping."

"That's the best thing for him right now."

Cora came out of the bedroom with her arms crossed. "I saw there was blood in his urine."

"I didn't want to say anything for fear he'd hear. How serious is that?"

"It could only be a bruise, or permanent damage. We'll have to wait and see."

Maggie took a seat at the kitchen table. "You both look exhausted."

"It's been really hard. Ronnie is in so much pain."

"Briggs went over and propped up Warren's door. He refused to put it back on the hinges. He said Warren deserved to freeze his ass off."

Cora sat down. "This is a mess."

Virgil leaned against the sink. "I'm staying here tonight. I'll be sleeping on the couch. I'm afraid Warren will wake up in the middle of the night and come looking for Ronnie. Cora is no match for that."

He ran his fingers through his hair. "Plus Jack is worried Warren will come in and take Ronnie."

"I think that's a great idea."

"I know there will be a lot of gossip."

"No there won't. I'll say I was here with you the whole time."

Cora's eyes widened. "Maggie, I can't ask you to lie."

"Then don't and let me do what I want."

"Can you take Jack to school tomorrow and on the way stop by and let Helen know I won't be in?"

"Sure, what else do you need?"

"Nothing that I can think of. I'm worried about tomorrow when Warren sobers up and finds Ronnie gone."

Virgil put his hand on hers and squeezed. "You let me deal with that."

CHAPTER TWENTY-ONE

Cora's head ached. She felt completely drained by the time Maggie left and Jack slept. "If you want to take your bath first, that's fine with me."

Virgil looked up from making his bed on the couch. "Are you sure you don't mind?"

"No, not at all. If Ronnie stays calm, I'm going to soak for a few minutes so I can fall asleep."

Virgil took his personal items and went into the bathroom. It felt strange yet reassuring that he was in her house, in her bathroom, and going to sleep on her couch. But mostly she was grateful that he'd be there should Warren come calling.

She couldn't deal with that and she would never give Ronnie up under any circumstance. If she had to run away with him she would. It would be hard, maybe impossible but she'd do what she had to do to protect Ronnie from his crazy father.

Soon Virgil came out wearing his trousers and a tee shirt but no shoes. "I'll wear my pants."

She shook her head. "I'm not that sensitive. Make yourself comfortable. Besides, we might be up all night with Ronnie."

"I don't want you to feel any more uncomfortable than you already are. I know this isn't the ideal situation for you."

"I worry about what the people of the town will say to the boys, but I can live with that if it protects Ronnie."

"You let me worry about the gossipers. I'm pretty good at putting people in their places."

She went into the bathroom. It was still warm and steamy from Virgil's bath. He'd cleaned the tub but the scent of his shaving cream, his razor on the top shelf of the sink and his comb all felt so intimate.

She wanted him so badly. She'd give anything for him to put his arms around her and make this entire problem go away. But he couldn't. Only time would tell how this situation would end.

The thought of losing Ronnie brought new tears to her eyes. She loved that poor, little boy who'd never know what it was like to have a mother's touch. All he had ever known was having a father that hated him and being a complete outcast.

Much like Pal.

She smiled when she thought of Jack. He had a good and honest heart. He'd take in or help anyone. He got that from his mother, Eleanor. How she missed her sister at times like this.

Relaxing back in the tub, she closed her eyes and thought of fonder times when Dan and Eleanor had first married. The "golden couple" they used to be called. Dan was on his way up in a successful career and Eleanor was the perfect woman at his side.

They lived in a beautiful house, they had elaborate parties and they both drove fancy cars. Both parents were as proud as they could be. Then like a knitted scarf, it all unraveled. Slowly at first, then like a freight train in the end.

That's why Cora would always blame Eleanor's murder on her parents. They were willing to do anything to remain in good standing in the community. Even sacrifice their youngest daughter, and now their grandson.

A knock startled her. "Yes?"

"Ronnie is awake. Is it time for his medicine?"

"I'm not sure. Is he crying?"

"More like a whimper."

"Try to get some cold milk down him and I'll be right out."

She dried off and grabbed her robe. Looking at the clock, she noted the medication would soon be wearing off and the pain would come roaring back.

Virgil had him on his knee, with a glass of milk to his lips. He drank thirstily for a while, and then he laid his head on Virgil's shoulder.

"I'll get the medicine. I'm giving it to him a little early, but by the time it kicks in, he might be able to go back to sleep."

"Did they say when we change the bandages on his back?"

"Not until tomorrow after a big dose of medicine."

Ronnie swallowed. Virgil carried him to the couch and gently hugged him against his chest. "You're going to be just fine, buddy."

Cora said, "I hope you're telling the truth."

Virgil looked at her, his eyes hard and bitter. "He'll be okay or his father will be dead."

She ran to the couch and sat beside him, clutching his arm. "Don't do that Virgil. Don't. Please promise me you won't."

"I can't promise you anything."

"Then what will happen to me and Jack and Ronnie if you go to jail?"

He put his arm around her and pulled her tightly against his side. She snuggled in closely and didn't want him to ever let go. Tears streamed down her cheeks and she rested her arm across the man and boy, afraid to let go.

He let out a deep breath. "This will all work out. I'll talk to the judge and I'll arrest Warren again. We'll see what the county commissioner has to say."

"Will they investigate?"

"Probably."

"Virgil, you do realize if Ronnie is taken away from Warren, the county will never give us custody of him."

"Why not?"

"I'm a convicted felon, a single mother of one child she can hardly afford to care for. Single women can't adopt children. They want them to go to a nice, normal family."

He kissed the top of Ronnie's head. "I guess that's not us."

"No, and it's entirely my fault. If you were married, I'm sure they'd consider you a great candidate. But, I have too much of a bad history to be considered a good parent."

"You're the best parent I know. Jack is taken care of and so is Ronnie. They couldn't ask for a better home life."

"That's not the way the courts will see it."

"What can we do?"

"You have to work tomorrow. I'm staying home to care for Ronnie, but I have to show up for work on Tuesday. Maybe Maggie will help with Ronnie until he can go to school."

"I was thinking I'd talk to the judge and get a statement from Dr. Lowery." He stood and carried the sleeping boy to the bedroom. "That's after I put Warren in jail."

"If you have time tomorrow, can you come by and watch Ronnie for a little while?"

"Sure. Where are you going?"

"To see JJ."

"He's colored. I doubt they'd let him represent us in court."

"He's a good person. He was my aunt's friend and he knows my past. At least he can give us some legal advice."

"Okay, if you think it will help."

"Ronnie's life is in danger. We have to try. I'm just hoping Ronnie is okay and somehow, someway we can prevent his father from hurting him again."

CHAPTER TWENTY-TWO

Virgil managed to get a better night's sleep than he expected. Ronnie slept through most of the night and the one time they did get up with him, it was because he had to use the restroom again.

Cora had given him a dose of medicine then and they'd settled back into sleep. When Virgil heard Ronnie whimpering, he went into the room, picked him up and brought him out to the living room where he slept on Virgil's chest. He knew it hurt too much for Ronnie to be on his back.

That's how Cora found them the next morning. She'd set the alarm to get Jack up for school, but before she roused him, she lifted Ronnie from Virgil's arms and put him back in his bed.

Virgil slipped on his trousers and raked his fingers through his hair. He quickly used the bathroom before Jack had to prepare for school.

Out in the kitchen, he put on a pot of coffee, then took a skillet off of the shelf and put a few slabs of bacon on to fry. He made a mental note to go by Howard Glover's today and buy groceries.

By the time Jack was washed and dressed for school, Virgil had his breakfast on the table along with his and Cora's. "I didn't know you could cook."

"You're seeing the extent of it right now."

Jack reluctantly left after being reassured Ronnie and Cora would be safe. Stopping to hug Pal, he ran out the door. Maggie stopped by the front porch where Cora waited. "How is Ronnie?"

"He's still pretty much out of it, but he had a good night."

"I'm glad to hear that."

Cora returned to the kitchen for another cup of coffee. Virgil went into the bathroom and came out with his hair combed, freshly shaved and wearing a clean uniform. Stomping into his boots he turned to leave.

"Today I'm calling the phone company. You need a phone for your protection and this way you can get in touch with me if something should happen."

"I can't let you pay for something like that."

"Why not?"

"It's not proper."

"Proper to who?"

"Everyone. We're probably already the talk of the town."

"I'm getting you a phone."

He left and she could tell by the stubborn set of his jaw, there'd be no changing his mind. She went about doing the dishes and cleaning up the kitchen. She made her bed and folded up the linen Virgil had used last night. She couldn't help bringing them to her nose to capture his scent.

The sky was cloudy and gray. Looking at Warren's house, she didn't see any sign he was up and about yet. She was near the back door when her neighbor knocked with his cane.

She answered with her finger to her lips. "Be quiet, Ronnie's still sleeping."

"Why ain't he in school?"

She explained what had happed and Earl's face grew stormier by the minute.

"I'm just hoping he'll be okay."

"I'm hoping someone has the guts to go over there and blow Warren's head off."

"That won't solve anything, Earl. Then the state would take Ronnie away."

"Well, you'd just have to adopt him."

"Not with my record. They'd never approve me and I'm single."

"You could marry the sheriff and end that problem."

"Not as simple as you think."

"I think you're the only one making it hard."

"This isn't about me and Virgil. I just want Ronnie safe and I want Warren to stop beating a defenseless child."

"He's been a rotten bastard since I've known him. His whole family's mean. I imagine Warren grew up much like Ronnie. His daddy was a drinker too."

"Monkey see, monkey do."

"What are we talking about monkeys for?"

"It's just an expression."

"Well, let's hope Virgil can come up with something. Somehow, we need to shut Warren down for good."

"If he'd willingly give up Ronnie, that might work, but he hates me and Virgil. He won't, though, just to spite us."

"Maybe we could buy him out."

She looked shocked. "We can't buy a child. I'm sure there are laws against that."

"How'd you get Jack?"

"His father gave up all rights to him. He had to go to court and get it signed by a judge for it to be legal for me to have custody."

"Can he get him back?"

"I don't think so. Also, Dan doesn't want anything to do with Jack."

Earl stood up. "Looks like the sheriff is about to deal with Warren."

Cora joined him at the window. "I hope Virgil doesn't hurt him."

"I hope he knocks him silly."

"Then he'll end up in jail."

"Who's going to tell?"

Luckily, it didn't come to that. Virgil moved the door aside, went in and came out with a squirming and kicking Warren Hayes by the collar. Virgil tossed him in the back seat and took off for the jail.

With him arrested, she didn't have to worry about him coming to her house and forcing his way in to get his son. That was too stressful. Now she just hoped someone, somehow could talk some sense into Warren.

"His ass is off to jail."

"I'm glad I don't have to worry about him coming here."

"He comes here, you give a holler, and I'll shoot his butt full of buckshot."

"That will only scare him away. He'd come back when you weren't looking."

"That wouldn't help him."

"I also worry, Earl, that he might hurt you. He's so angry and bitter."

"Well, maybe something will change. I need to get back home." He stood. "I finished that cobbler by the way. It was pretty good. You still need to keep practicing, but you're getting there."

She smiled. "So, you'd like to try something else?"

He walked out the door and said over his shoulder, "I'm all about second chances."

She saw Maggie returning from school and waved. "Thanks for taking Jack to school."

"I explained to Miss Potter that Ronnie wasn't coming for a few days. I insisted she tell me what she told Warren to prompt him to beat his child senseless."

"What did she say?"

"Claims to be completely innocent. Said she barely mentioned anything."

"That might be true. It doesn't take much to make Warren mad."

"Or the bitch could be lying through her teeth. For some reason I don't like her."

"She's okay. She gave me a bit of a problem when she heard the latest gossip, but I set her straight and since then she's been nice."

"Well, she sent a report card. She shouldn't have said anything to Warren."

"I'm wondering if Ronnie got that beating because I hadn't taken Warren the report card yet. It could all very well be my fault."

Maggie touched her arm. "Nothing is your fault. That man is sick and needs his brains bashed in."

"I just wonder what Virgil's going to do. He took him in earlier."

"Yeah, they passed me on the way home and Warren didn't look too happy."

"I doubt he's even sober yet."

"I don't know what we can do. I just want you to know, if there's anything me or my family can do to help you in any way, just say the word."

She hugged Maggie. "You're a wonderful friend."

"I don't know about that, but you've loved Ronnie like he was your own and that says something about the kind of person you are."

Cora went back into the house and checked on Ronnie. His left eye blinked open a little so she moved closer. "Are you okay?"

"I think so. It hurts."

"I know and moving around will only hurt more, but you need to eat. Are you hungry?"

He rubbed his cheek. "My jaw hurts too much."

"I know. But all you've had is a little milk."

"My tummy doesn't feel good. Is the sheriff here?"

"No, he's at work, but if you need to go to the bathroom I can help you."

He slowly shook his head. "I'm okay. Will he come soon?"

Now she wished she had the damn phone. "Hold on just a minute. She ran out the back door and knocked on Earl's door.

"What's the matter?"

"Ronnie has to use the restroom and he's too shy to let me help him and I don't know when Virgil will return."

"I'll be right there."

Earl arrived a few minutes after she came in. Cora lifted Ronnie and stood him in the bathroom with Earl, then closed the door.

Once he was finished, she picked him up and put him back in bed. "Thank you so much, Earl. I don't know why he's so shy."

"He a young boy, that's why." Earl washed his hands. "No one his age wants a girl to see his wiener."

"Jack isn't that crazy about it either."

"You have to respect a young man's modesty."

"I'll watch that. Now I wish they were girls."

"Be glad they're polite enough to know how to behave in front of a female."

She walked him to the back door. "I guess you're right."

"Damn right, I am."

She went to the bedroom with a basin of warm water, a clean wash cloth and fresh bandages. She gave him a dose of medicine and then slowly removed his shirt and the covering over his wounds.

Her head spun and she nearly lost her breakfast when she saw the damage done by Warren. In an instant she wanted to shoot him too. Ronnie shivered in pain and whimpered.

She hated the thought of hurting him. A knock sounded at the door and she ran to open it. She was relieved to see Virgil at the door. "I'm trying to change the bandages, can you help?"

He followed her and sat on the edge of the bed holding Ronnie's hand. His face tightened when he saw the damage done to the little boy's back. "Hey buddy. You feel better today?"

"I don't hurt as much as I did in the hospital."

"I'm surprised you remember that."

"I remember because it hurt so bad."

"Aunt Cora has to change the bandages. It might be uncomfortable, but she'll be real fast."

Ronnie gripped the pillow and squeezed his eyes shut.

Cora did work quickly. She washed the wounds, applied the salve and covered the area. So far nothing was infected, which was good, and he wasn't running a temperature. With any luck he'd pull out of this okay. But, he'd probably be physically and emotionally scarred for the rest of his life.

Virgil knelt beside the bed and rubbed Ronnie's head while he cried. Soon it was over. Virgil picked him up and walked the floor with the little boy in his arms. Ronnie turned his face into Virgil's neck, cuddling closer.

Cora cleaned up the mess left by dressing the wounds and hurried into the kitchen where she broke down crying. She collapsed at the table. Leaning forward on the table, she buried her face in her arms and cried.

A slight noise alerted her that Virgil stood beside her, Ronnie asleep against his shoulder. "Help me get him to bed."

She brushed her tears aside and ran to straighten the bed. When the sheet was righted and the pillow fluffed, she slipped a clean pajama top on Ronnie then they tucked him into bed. Virgil gathered her in his arms and squeezed tightly.

She sobbed until the front of his shirt was soaked, then she backed away and went into the bathroom and washed her face. She came out to see Virgil had put a bag on the table she hadn't seen earlier.

"What's this?"

"I knew you were too exhausted to think of food, so I stopped by Betty's and grabbed us a couple of sandwiches."

"That's very kind of you."

He took the food out of the bag and placed a roast beef sandwich in front of her, then took his own out of the sack. Before sitting down, he fixed them both a glass of iced tea.

She took a bite and realized she was hungrier than she thought. She'd been so concerned about Ronnie not eating she'd forgotten about herself.

"Did Warren have anything to say when you took him to the station?"

"He did a lot of threatening, cussing and blowing off steam, but that was about it."

"He's in jail, right?"

"Yes, I had the judge come over because Warren was threatening to file charges against us for taking Ronnie to the hospital without his permission. The judge ruled he was too drunk to make a reasonable decision."

"How long is he locked up?"

"At least the next seventy-two hours. Judge wants to come by and see Ronnie's injuries for himself. He also called the hospital. He's trying to prove we acted in the best interest of the child."

"Was there any doubt?"

"Warren says we kidnapped Ronnie. We broke into his house and stole his child."

She pushed her sandwich aside. "The nerve of the man."

"That's what I thought too, but he is correct in the fact that I knocked down his door and took Ronnie."

"Do you have jurisdiction to do that?"

"Only if the child's life is in danger." He took a bite of his sandwich and chewed slowly. She could tell he wasn't any more interested in his food than she was hers.

"Well, the doctor should agree that was the case."

"I'm sure he will."

She touched his hand. "Are you worried?"

"I'm worried that Warren will somehow manage to get his hands on Ronnie again. I think if that happens, he'll kill him."

CHAPTER TWENTY-THREE

Virgil wasn't sure the sandwich would stay in his stomach. The image of Ronnie's bloody back nearly sickened him to the point he wanted to hurt someone.

"Let's stay within the law. I love Ronnie with all my heart and I'd give anything to keep him here where he's safe forever, but I have to think of Jack. If there is too much attention directed at me, my parole could be violated and I might be sent back to prison."

"I'm not going to let that happen."

"Are you sure you can stop it?"

"I'm sure I can put up a helluva good fight."

"That might not be enough."

A knock sounded at the door and Virgil stood. "That's probably the judge."

Judge Garner came in and Virgil introduced him to Cora. "You're welcome to half my sandwich. I didn't touch it."

"No thank you, Miss Williams."

"How about I put on a pot of coffee?" She moved toward the sink. "I have some leftover apple-pecan pie, if you'd like a piece."

"That sounds wonderful and my sweet tooth is too big to turn down a handsome offer."

"Come on in."

Virgil cleaned off the table and took out three cups and plates for pie. As the coffee perked, Judge Garner asked Virgil to show him Ronnie.

Cora stayed in the kitchen and he was glad. She'd been so upset he feared she'd be a wreck by the time all this ended. They went into the bedroom. Virgil turned on the light switch and looked at Ronnie, who lay on his stomach.

Gently pulling back the covers, he lifted the shirt and peeled off the bandages to expose the horrible wounds. He heard the judge's sharp intake of breath. Then he showed him the bruises on his arms, and pulled down his pajama bottoms and little underwear to see more welts, bloody cuts, and massive bruises on Ronnie's legs.

When Virgil turned him over, Ronnie moaned. But he lay still as he showed the injuries to the front of his body. The judge didn't say anything as Virgil covered Ronnie and turned off the light.

"Cora's been putting ice cold cloths on his face to help the swelling."

"Does his face look better today?"

"Yes. I think so."

"Then I can only imagine what it looked like last night."

The darkness in the judge's eyes clearly let Virgil know how angry Judge Garner was because he felt the same way. His hands slightly trembled as his lifted his cup.

"When does he go back to Dr. Lowery?"

"Tomorrow afternoon." Cora cleared her throat. "I think he'll suggest we cut back on the pain medication and leave the bandages off to encourage scabbing so the wounds will heal quicker."

"You're a doctor, Miss Williams. How do you think the child will do after this is all over?"

She wrung her hands. "Children are terribly resilient and they heal faster than adults. If there aren't any internal injuries, his body may heal, but he'll be scarred."

"Mentally?"

"It's going to take a lot to keep Ronnie secure and make him feel safe. He's frightened his father will come and get him and it will be hard to get him out of the house away from me or Virgil."

"Do you think there have been internal injuries?"

"Some bruising that will eventually heal, and there was blood in his urine, but it's cleared up. That's a good sign."

She stood and served the pie while Virgil poured the coffee.

"This is a tough case."

Virgil blew on his hot coffee. "We were just talking about that. And Cora has every right to be worried about Jack. His father gave her custody, but we're not sure he can't fight that at some time."

"As a judge, you both know I can't give you legal advice. I wanted to see for myself that Ronnie was severely beaten enough that I could press charges and keep Warren in jail for up to ten days."

"Then what?"

"He has every right to get a lawyer and take you both to court."

Cora glanced in the direction of the small bedroom. "That's what I'm afraid of. With my past, I won't stand up under scrutiny."

"You have a real concern there. People are good at making their own assumptions. A woman who's spent time in prison has a mark against her going in."

"So what do we do?"

"I'm going to sentence Warren to jail for ten days. By then Ronnie will be on the mend. I'm very reluctant to call in the child protective agency because sometimes they make it more complicated because protocol mandates that they immediately take the child and put him in an orphanage."

Cora gasped. "No, I don't want Ronnie to go into a place like that."

The judge finished his pie, commented on what a good cook she was and then took his leave. Virgil knew the judge couldn't do much, but at least Warren was behind bars for the next ten days.

"Well, we're going to have to come up with something."

"I can't imagine what, Virgil. I can't change my past."

"Something will happen. Maybe Warren will have a change of heart."

She scoffed. "You're joking now."

"Who knows? Let's just take it one day at a time."

"At least we have ten days."

"And we can always pray that Warren will change his mind."

"I'm not counting on anything good coming from that guy. Anyone who'd do what he did to a child should be put in front of a firing squad."

Virgil chuckled. "I agree."

A knock sounded at the door. Cora rubbed her forehead. "I think I get more company than anyone in town."

She opened the door and Reverend Fuller stood there with his wife, Edith. "Hello," she said not sure what to think. "Can I help you?"

The preacher stepped forward. "We've heard a great tragedy has happened to little Ronnie Hayes and we wanted to come by and see if there was anything you need."

Virgil's gaze fell to the linen folded on the couch. If Fuller saw that and put things together, he'd create a scandal...again.

Charles and Edith practically pushed themselves into the living room. The reverend's wife shoved a pan of food at Cora. "I thought I'd help out by fixing a meal. Nothing keeps a woman busier than tending a sick child."

"Ronnie isn't sick, he was severely beaten."

"That was brought to my attention and I plan to visit Warren at the jail this afternoon and let him know that a Godly man doesn't beat a child so badly he goes to the hospital."

Virgil went into the living room and took the food from Cora's hands. "We'd invite you in but with Ronnie being so sick, Miss Williams is exhausted."

Then he backed them out of the house. If they thought they were going to come here and gawk at a beaten and battered child, they were crazy. He wouldn't tolerate it for one minute.

When they reached the porch, Virgil kicked the door shut.

Cora stared at him, her mouth wide open. "Virgil, that was rude."

"No, they're rude. I don't want those hypocrites in this house. Not after what he said to you."

She took the casserole and walked toward the kitchen. "He apologized."

"After Maggie threatened to beat him to death with her rolling pin."

"They probably meant well."

"I seriously doubt that. My guess is they saw my squad car out front and are far more interested in what we're doing than what's going on with Ronnie."

"He said he was going to talk to Warren. Do you think it will do any good?"

"Ronnie has been abused most of his life. Not like last night, but his dad's always been brutal to the boy. No one cared until you came along. Maggie helped some, Helen took a few meals over there. A couple of times Mae made sure Ronnie had something to eat." He pulled out a chair and sat at the table. "No one brought that child into their home and loved him like you have."

"He was just so neglected."

"He was, but you're the only one who really cared. So, the people in this town better watch what they say about this whole situation or I'll start locking people up."

She rubbed his strong shoulders. "You're a good man, Virgil Wade Carter."

"Right now, I'm just really pissed."

"Can you stay for a few minutes?"

"Sure, why?"

"I want to talk to JJ. He's smart and he can give legal advice. I feel in my heart that if he can help us, he will."

CHAPTER TWENTY-FOUR

Cora went to the bathroom and freshened up a little before putting on a jacket and going to the door. "I won't be long."

Cora arrived at JJ's office and waited about twenty minutes before he had time to see her. She embraced him fondly. "I don't know if you've heard about Ronnie Hayes."

"Yes, Nell told my wife and she told me. We're very sorry to hear such a horrible thing."

"I have Ronnie right now, but I'm afraid his father will eventually get him back."

JJ took her arm and led her to a chair. He sat next to her. "Cora, the law is on the parent's side. Courts, juries, and even the churches don't want to see a family split apart. No matter how dysfunctional the family may be."

"That means that after Warren serves his ten days he can come and take Ronnie away and there's nothing we can do?"

"Have you spoken to Warren?"

Shaking her head, Cora said, "Very little." She looked away, fighting the tears. "He hates Virgil."

"There's no hope he'd turn over custody to you?"

Again, she shook her head. "Highly unlikely."

"With you having served a prison sentence, the last thing we want this to do is go to trial."

"Today Judge Garner came to see the injuries to Ronnie himself. Him seeing Ronnie's wounds, and Dr. Lowery's statement, allowed him to sentence Warren to jail for ten days."

JJ took her hand. "That gives us time, Cora."

"But the judge said Warren could still fight to have Virgil charged with breaking into his house and kidnapping Ronnie."

"Now, that's true. But, remember, there aren't many people in this community who don't know that Warren is a brute and a drunk. While on the other hand, Virgil Carter is an honest, decorated war veteran. No lawyer will touch that case."

Her shoulders slumped. "I'm so glad to see Virgil won't get in trouble."

"Also, the judge is very fond of Virgil. Always has been." JJ took her other hand. "What about you and Virgil. Is there anything there?"

She knew what he meant. "We haven't done anything."

"That's not my business and not the question. Do you care for him?"

Tears hung on the edge of her lower lashes. "I could really love a man like Virgil. He's wonderful and the boys love him." She pulled from his grasp. "JJ, you're my friend. I feel I've known you all my life and I'm comfortable confiding in you."

She stood and paced the floor. "Things happened in prison I can never undo. Horrible things that make me feel I'll never be clean again. Virgil deserves better than that."

JJ stood and hugged her tenderly. "You're always thinking about all the people around you who need love, but you don't think yourself worthy. Let Virgil be the judge of what he deserves."

"JJ, I didn't come to talk about Virgil and me, what about Ronnie?"

"I don't have an immediate answer. Warren isn't a man who cares what the community thinks about him, so his past is safe. I don't think if he's determined for Virgil not to have the child, he can be bought. That means we have to find out what Warren wants."

"I don't understand."

JJ smiled, his dark face filled with warmth. "I have a man who does some investigating for me. Let me see what he can find."

"Let me know what I owe you. Whatever it is, I'll find a way to pay you."

JJ reared back. "Now you're insulting me."

"I can't expect you to work at no cost."

"Why not?"

"This is how you make a living, JJ. I can't deprive you of that."

"You mean a great deal to me, Cora. You saved Betsy Ford's life. I think I can do a little checking around for you."

She kissed his cheek. "I'll check back with you in a few days."

"My wife will kill me if I don't ask you if you need anything."

"That's kind, but I'm fine. I just need Ronnie to heal."

"If you need someone to care for him, Nell's older sister is wonderful with children."

"Thank you, for everything."

She left and stopped by the dry cleaners. Helen, Ma Baker and Nell were all questions. They were concerned about Ronnie and wanted to help her in any way they could.

"I think it's going to be okay. Ronnie goes back to the doctor tomorrow. I plan to come to work Wednesday."

Helen came closer and hugged her tightly. "You take all the time you need."

"What I need is to continue earning a salary."

"We'll take care of that. I spoke with Mrs. Cooper and she said to pay you for two days. So, don't worry."

"I know you are all taking up the slack and I hate to burden you with more work."

Helen patted her arm. "You take care of Ronnie."

Nell came over. "Is that Warren going to prison?"

Cora shook her head. "No, the judge sentenced him to ten days in jail."

"Is that all? For almost killing a child?"

"I know, but I guess being a parent gives you the right to do whatever you want to a child."

Ma Baker shook her head. "There should be laws that protect children."

Nell said, "There should be something Virgil can do to Warren to keep him from hurting that baby."

"I went to JJ earlier and asked for his advice. He's going to see what he can do."

Helen touched Cora's shoulder. "We were talking earlier about you adopting Ronnie, but I bet they won't let you."

"No, there isn't a chance."

She left the ladies at the dry cleaners and walked into her house to find Virgil sitting on the couch with Ronnie in his arms. "Did he wake up?"

"Just for a minute. He was thirsty."

"Did he get fussy?"

"No."

"Then why isn't he in bed?"

Virgil patted his bottom. "Because I just want to hold him."

That touched her deeply. Virgil loved Ronnie as much as she did. How could they ever let him go? She'd never be able to stay in this house and wonder what agony Ronnie might be going through. It'd kill her.

She rubbed Ronnie's arm. "Bless his heart. He's such a strong boy."

"I know. And he asks for so little."

"I don't think he's ever asked for anything, even when I knew he was hungry."

"Yeah, he's just a good boy all around."

"I hope we get good news from the doctor tomorrow."

"His face looks better. When I gave him a drink, he could open both his eyes."

"That's good."

"I better put him back to bed. I have to get to the station." He made his way into the bedroom. He came out and handed her a slip of paper. "The phone man came while you were gone." He pointed to the black cradle phone on the table next to the chair. "This is your new number and it should be all connected tomorrow."

"Your number?"

He pointed to the note. "It's on the back."

"I feel bad that you paid for the phone when it's in my house." She thought of the guard Grubber and wondered if he'd come back and feared his threat was valid.

"I can't go out there and do my job not knowing if you're safe."

"Will you be back for dinner?"

"Yes, I have several things to do first."

Cora stayed busy until Jack came home, his usual self, full of energy and because he didn't know the extent of Ronnie's injuries, wondered why he couldn't play.

"Aunt Cora is that a phone?"

"Yes, Virgil had it put in today. The man will be here to hook it up tomorrow."

"That's gonna be fun when it rings. Can I answer it?"

"If you're polite."

"I wish Ronnie could play," Jack said with a frown. "How come he has to stay in bed so long?"

"He's healing."

He put a stack of papers on the table. Bright pictures were drawn in crayons. "Miss Potter had the class color get well cards for Ronnie and she gave them to me to bring home."

"That will put a smile to his face."

"What's a get well card?"

"It's just a note, or in this case, a picture that helps a person who is sick feel better."

"So, it's like medicine?"

"Medicine for the heart." She ruffled his hair. "It's a kind gesture."

"Good, if Ronnie feels better, me and Tommy feel better too."

"That's good. How was school today?"

"It was fun. We went out for recess and I made it all the way across the monkey bars."

"My, aren't you getting strong."

Jack raised his fists and tried to squeeze his biceps. "I'm going to be as strong as Virgil someday."

"There is no doubt about that."

Tommy appeared at the back door. "Hi, Miss Cora. Can I come in?"

"Sure, Tommy."

"My mom said if I get too loud you can send me home."

Cora smiled, happy at the thought that at least Jack and Tommy were healthy and happy little boys. Ronnie was another story completely.

She silently prayed JJ could come up with something that would help the situation, but honestly, she held out little hope. What could convince a tyrant like Warren to put his child in a place where he'd be loved and cared for?

Virgil came in using the key she'd given him. She didn't want to be at work and him not able to get in. He didn't look happy. She imagined it was because he had to listen to Warren scream and threaten all day.

"You look gloomy."

"I'm just worried about Ronnie."

"I am too, but he seems to be getting better."

"Good, I hope the doctor has good news tomorrow."

Tommy and Jack ran to greet Virgil. Jack jumped into his arms and hugged him while Tommy showed him a big cats-eye marble that had magical powers. No one could beat him with that.

Tommy soon left for home while Cora placed plates on the table. She'd made a hearty stew and cornbread. As they sat down to eat, Ronnie shuffled out of the bedroom.

"I'm hungry."

His little face was bruised, but most of the swelling had gone down, and the cut above his eyes looked better. Virgil went to him and knelt. "Do you have to go to the bathroom first?"

Ronnie nodded.

"Do you need my help?"

"I can do it myself, I think."

Virgil put his hand on the boy's shoulder and led him to the bathroom. "I'll just wait out here should you need me."

While Virgil waited, Cora went into the bedroom and took out a clean pair of socks. "He'll need to keep his feet warm."

Virgil helped Ronnie wash his hands then put the socks on his feet and guided him to the table. He still wasn't steady.

Cora set out a small bowl of creamy potato soup she'd made just for Ronnie. That would be the most nourishing and the easiest to chew.

His movements were slow but he managed to clean his bowl and drain a half glass of milk.

Cora took his bowl and looked at Jack. "Don't you have something for Ronnie?"

Jack jumped up and ran to the table near the front door. "Look, Ronnie. We all colored you get well cards at school today."

Ronnie's eyes grew. "Wow, are all these for me?"

"Yes, Aunt Cora said they'll make you get well."

Ronnie looked at each picture and smiled. "They're pretty."

"I know." Jack pulled one from the pile. "This one's mine." There were two little boys standing in front of a house with a big sun in the right corner. "That's you and me."

"It looks like us, Jack. You sure can draw good."

"I know."

Cora looked across at Virgil who smiled along with the boys. Ronnie had managed to crawl up on Virgil's lap and was content to show him every picture.

"There are some really talented artists in your class."

"I like Jack's best."

Virgil tilted his head and looked at the picture. "I think you're right. I like it best too." He glanced at Cora. "Maybe we can put this one on your wall in the bedroom so you can see it when you wake up."

Cora nodded her approval.

While she finished the dishes, Virgil had the boys on the couch listening to a radio program. She came in with a steaming cup of coffee and a plate of sugar cookies she'd made earlier as a surprise.

The boys dug in and Virgil didn't seem to mind them crawling all over him while they moved around the couch. He only put his hand up to stop Jack once when he became a little overzealous and starting roughhousing with Ronnie, who simply didn't have the energy.

Pal laid on the rug, lifting his head occasionally to check out his surroundings. Several times he stood up, put his head in Ronnie's lap and licked his face.

Before long Jack was in the tub and Ronnie was struggling to keep awake in Virgil's lap.

She put her hand on his shoulder. "When Jack finishes, it's time to change the bandages again."

Ronnie protested.

"It's okay, the medicine will help."

"I don't like that medicine. It tastes bad."

"Maybe you won't have to take it much longer."

"When can I go back to school?"

"We have to wait and see what the doctor says."

Ronnie whined. "I don't want to go to the doctor. I don't like it there."

"You want to go back to school and be outside playing with Tommy and Jack, don't you?"

"Yes."

"Seeing the doctor is how we make that possible. Now take your medicine like a big boy."

When Jack finished and they'd put him to bed in with her again, Cora and Virgil took Ronnie to the bathroom and sat him on the toilet with the seat down. She filled the basin with warm water. As she reached to remove the wrappings on his back, he reached out and encircled Virgil's legs with his skinny arms and buried his face in his thighs.

"Get it over as fast as you can." Virgil rubbed his head. "He's trembling already."

She made fast work of tending to his wounds and before long they had Ronnie tucked in bed, complaining he wanted to sleep on the couch with Virgil.

"You'll sleep better in here. But, Virgil is right there in the living room. He's not going anywhere."

After they returned to the kitchen, Virgil looked out the window at Warren's house. "I'd love to walk into the jail and blow that man's head off."

CHAPTER TWENTY-FIVE

Virgil and Cora had taken Ronnie to the doctor and he was healing nicely. Today he was able to return to school and they only had two days before Warren would be released.

Cora had been so frightened that his dad would hurt the child again that she was talking about running away with him and Jack.

Of course, she couldn't do that. He simply wouldn't allow that and all he had to mention was Jack could be taken away and her thoughts became rational again.

He returned to his office only to find the small space filled with women. Close to twenty. The deputy stood between them and the door to the jail.

"What's going on here, John?"

Sweating, his shirt torn and hair messed up, John replied. "I think they plan to lynch Warren."

Nell turned around and faced him. "No, we don't want to hang him. That's too good for him." She held up an empty bottle. "We just want to talk to him."

"Yeah," the teacher, Ruth Potter, agreed shaking her ruler.

Maggie, with her rolling pin, pushed to the front of the crowd. "We're here to help Warren decide to let Cora adopt Ronnie."

Virgil held up his hands. "Ladies, I'm proud of each of you for taking an interest in Ronnie's welfare. However, I can't let you persuade a prisoner to do anything."

"Why not?" Ester shouted. "He's a child beater."

"Whatever he is will be decided by the courts. I want you ladies to put your weapons away and if you feel you have to do something, express your concern to Judge Garner."

Grumbling, they reluctantly filed out of his office and marched like new recruits to the courthouse. John stepped closer, wiped his brow then looked out the window. "Phew, I have to say, I thought they'd overpower me."

"All those women surprise me. Usually they mind their own business and we never hear a peep out of them." Virgil shook his head. "Even Miss Caroline Dixon was with them. She's the quietest person I know. It must take a lot to get her riled up."

"Yeah, she's always been like a church mouse."

"I don't think that. When your daddy is Big Jim Dixon, it's probably hard to live up to that boisterous personality."

John looked away. "I really liked Big Jim. When he died, I think half the life went out of Gibbs City."

"It was a sad day for all of us. Especially Caroline. She was the apple of her daddy's eye."

"Yeah, then her momma goes off and marries some man half her age."

"That's none of our business."

John straightened his shirt. "I wish the women of this town would go back to cooking and cleaning. I honestly think they came here to do Warren bodily harm."

"That's possible."

"I wonder if I would've stopped them."

Virgil gripped John by the shoulder. "Of course you would. Never doubt doing the right thing."

Several hours later Virgil received a call from the judge. He'd half expected that after sending half the female citizens to his office. As he made his way there, he ran into JJ. "Where are you off to?"

JJ smiled and patted him on the shoulder. "I'm meeting with the judge, just like you."

"I hope its good news."

"Only the big man can determine that."

Inside the building, they removed their hats and climbed the stairs to the second floor. After waiting a few minutes, they were called into the judge's chambers.

"Good afternoon, gentlemen."

Virgil didn't like the stern expression on his friend's face. "What's going on, Judge?"

"As if you didn't know."

"I simply aimed the citizens in a direction where they could voice their concerns." He held out his hands. "I'm just the sheriff. My job is to uphold the law."

"That and sic a bunch of women on a defenseless judge."

JJ grinned. "You do that, Virgil?"

The judge threw a folder on his desk. "Hell yes, he did."

Virgil shrugged and fought back a grin.

"I want to talk to both of you about Ronnie Hayes."

Virgil struggled to remain calm. The stern expression on the man behind the desk didn't help alleviate Virgil's tension.

"Why is JJ here?"

"Because he's investigating every possible angle he can to get Warren to do the right thing and agree to surrender Ronnie to Cora."

Virgil frowned. "So it's not a good sign that we're gathering here."

"That depends on how you look at things. Let's all assume that Ronnie's happiness and safety come before anything else."

Virgil and JJ nodded.

"I had John bring Warren to my office earlier today. I spoke with him and he made several things clear."

JJ folded his arms. "I bet he did."

"One, he refused to give up Ronnie." The judge pointed to Virgil. "Especially not to you or Cora. Second, he's still angry and feels he's been mistreated by the justice system and thinks beating his child isn't anyone's business." The judge looked down. "He also plans to continue treating Ronnie the way he always has."

Virgil bristled. "That bastard."

"He has to go to jail," JJ said. "He's going to kill that child."

"That's brought me to my decision. I've decided I'm filing charges against Warren Hayes for endangerment of a child."

"That means the state will take Ronnie."

The judge held up his hand. "That's correct, but Warren won't be able to hurt him anymore because he'll serve at least three years."

JJ shoved back his chair. "So, Ronnie still loses?"

"Maybe not."

Virgil stood up. "How can this help Ronnie or Cora?"

Judge Garner cleared his throat. "I'm very fond of Miss Williams, but this isn't about her."

"Then what is it about?"

"Doing what's best for Ronnie."

"How?" Virgil paced. "By putting him in an orphanage with strangers where he stands a good chance of being treated as badly as he was at his dad's hands?"

"No, Ronnie will become a ward of the state and adopted."

Virgil wondered if he heard correctly. "By who?"

"It can't be Miss Williams. The state has made that clear."

"We knew that. Not with her record."

"Let me have my say, Virgil."

"There is a couple here, in Gibbs City, who has been waiting two years to adopt a child. As the ladies of the community so graciously brought to my attention." Judge leaned back. "They would immediately become his foster parents then when all the paperwork goes through Ronnie would become their adoptive son."

JJ sat up. "Who are these people?"

"Benjamin and Susan Welsh."

Virgil leaned across the judge's desk. "The pharmacist?"

"Yes, he and Susan can't have children, so they turned to adoption but the wait is horrendous. I've talked to the State Representative and that office agreed to push the legal documents forward due to Ronnie's physical injuries."

It solved all the problems except Cora. JJ and Virgil exchanged a concerned look.

"She's not going to be happy," JJ warned.

"I know. It'll crush her to give up Ronnie."

The judge stood. "Helping her understand is your job, Virgil."

"Thanks."

"The Welsh's would love to meet Ronnie as soon as possible, but they're very sensitive to your and Cora's feeling for the child."

Virgil and JJ left, only to stop outside the courthouse.

JJ grasped his arm. "Do you want me to go with you?"

"No, but don't leave town, I may need you later."

As Virgil walked to his office, he mentally tried to practice the words he'd use to convince Cora everything would be okay and this was all for the best. The problem was he couldn't quite convince himself.

He'd miss Ronnie. After days and nights of helping him through all the pain and suffering he'd been through, how could he let him go?

And there was Jack. He practically considered Ronnie his brother. How would he react to all this? How would Ronnie react to being sent to stay with someone else?

He looked at the clock tower. Cora had two more hours before she'd be off work. He decided it was best if he talked to her before dinner.

He went to Maggie's. She came to the door smiling. "Come on in, Virgil. You want a hot cup of coffee?"

"That sounds good."

He closed the door and walked into the warm kitchen to the aroma of stew cooking. After removing his hat and shedding his jacket, he took a seat.

She placed two cups on the table and sat across from him. "I expected you."

"You ladies went right to the judge's office."

Maggie nodded firmly, obviously feeling no shame at their action. "Something had to be done and Cora gave us the courage to see how standing on the sidelines wasn't helping Ronnie."

"She's still not going to like Ronnie going to the Welsh's."

"We all put our heads together. We wanted Cora to have Ronnie, but we ran into a roadblock with her past." Maggie stood and refiled her cup. "We scoured the town for someone else he could go to and still be in Cora's life."

"You came up with Benjamin and Susan Welsh?"

"Yes. They are wonderful people who desperately want a child. They're thrilled at the possibility of adopting Ronnie. And this way he won't go into the system."

"It's going to break Cora's heart."

Maggie leaned forward with a frown. "It will, but the alternative is Ronnie being taken completely away."

"The judge is on board with the Welsh's and they do live here in Gibbs City."

Maggie took a sip of her coffee and then looked out the window. "I know losing Ronnie will crush both of you, but they're good people, Virgil."

"I don't know them personally, but any time I've encountered them they've seemed nice."

"She teaches Sunday school, and when Floyd and Doris's house burned down, Susan was right there donating boxes of food and even clothing. Items she'd purchased for the children."

"It's not that I think they're bad people, Maggie. It's that they aren't us."

"Cora's going to be upset." Maggie put her hand on Virgil's arm. "Listen to me. Cora loves Ronnie as if he was her own, but she's already struggling to support herself and Jack."

When he went to tell her that he'd help, she held out her hand. "Cora has Jack and that's all she needs. Ronnie will be in a nice, safe house with people who'll love him. And they only live a block and a half away." She patted his hand. "Cora could see him every day."

"I understand what you're saying, but put all that aside, all Cora's going to hear is that she's losing Ronnie."

"I can't say I envy you. You've got a hard row to plow, but you have to make her understand that Jack needs her and she has to let Ronnie go."

"Will you watch the boys after school while I talk to her?"

He stood, and Maggie put her hand on his back. "Of course I will. I've made plenty of stew. I'll feed them supper before I send them home."

He hugged her. "Thanks."

"Hey, when are you going to marry that woman?"

Virgil opened the door and put on his coat. "Don't even open that can of worms."

CHAPTER TWENTY-SIX

Cora left work anxious to see how the boys' day at school went. She was reluctant to let Ronnie go today, but he was doing so much better and sitting at home without his friends wasn't much fun.

When she got to the corner, Virgil stood waiting for her. She smiled. Was there ever a man so handsome and caring? During his time with them, he'd shown such a tender side she couldn't help but think about him all day.

"Are you as excited as I am to see how the day went for the boys?"

He took her arm and continued down the street. "Let's stop by Betty's and have a piece of pie and coffee."

"But the kids are due home from school and I need to start dinner."

He clutched her tighter. "Maggie has the boys."

She stopped in the middle of the sidewalk and forced him to face her. "What's wrong?"

"Nothing." He shuffled his feet then looked into her eyes. "Everything."

"Is it Ronnie?"

Tears pressed against the back of her eyes. Her heart stopped and her chest constricted. The sad look on Virgil's face spoke to her heart, begging it not to break.

"It isn't necessarily bad."

"What?" She grabbed his arm and shook him. "What's going on?"

"JJ and I spoke with Judge Garner today. A decision has been made."

Her stomach turned, perspiration dampened her back and she struggled to breathe. She pulled at the scarf around her neck, and unbuttoned her coat, trying to get more air into her lungs. "They're taking him, aren't they?" Tears ran down her cheeks. "He's not ours anymore."

Virgil pulled her close and rubbed her back, but that wasn't what she wanted. She wanted a helpless child who needed to be loved and cared for. She shoved him away and wiped at her face.

"Warren is going to jail and Ronnie is being turned over to the state."

Physical pain shot through her entire body and agony pierced her skin like daggers. She could barely stand. It wasn't fair. Not to Ronnie, not to her.

God, where was the justice in this world?

"When does he leave?"

"There's a couple here in Gibbs City who has been trying to adopt a child for years. The state has agreed to let them foster Ronnie until the adoption papers can be filed." He touched her cheek. That's when she noticed the dampness in his eyes. "He'll live right here in town and we can see him every day."

"Who are these people? Do you know them? Are they good parents? Will they care for him like we did?" Her voice rose to a shout. She lowered her gaze when several people walking by glanced at them. Now she felt like a screaming maniac.

They were taking her child.

"Cora, we have to consider what's best for Ronnie. He deserves two parents, a family and a future."

"I'll marry you. I'll marry you today." She stood on her toes, clutching the lapels of his jacket. "Then he can be ours."

Virgil shook his head. "Not with your past. The judge promised me he tried to get you custody. They wouldn't go for it."

Her.

She was the reason Ronnie had to go live with strangers. Be torn from a home where people loved him. The tears ran freely as she clutched her stomach and bent over from the staggering pain.

"It's my fault."

Virgil grabbed her in his tight grasp. "Cora, let's think of Ronnie. I know this hurts you. It hurts me, too. And Jack will be disappointed. But, these people will be good for Ronnie."

"How do you know?"

"I've checked them out. It's the pharmacist and his wife Susan."

Cora's gaze swung to the drugstore as if by looking there she'd see the villain who wanted the child she cared for.

"When?"

"Cora, there's time."

She shoved away from him and balled her fists.

Anger so raw and violent reared up inside her, powerful enough to melt the sidewalks. "When?" she screamed. "When do I have to give him up?"

"Cora."

He reached for her but she slapped at his outstretched hands. "Don't touch me."

She ran away as fast as she could. Down Main Street, all the way home. Once at her porch, she slumped on the front steps, exhausted. JJ sat waiting. "You know?"

"Yes, and I'm here to help if you'll let me."

"How can I let them take him from me?"

"It's hard."

"JJ, you're a man. You don't know the heart of a mother."

"Let me tell you a little story. There was once a beautiful woman who fell in love with a man of color. She became pregnant. Now in this world this doesn't end well. So the couple decided that if the child was born white, the mother would take and raise the little boy and claim he was a nephew. If the little boy was black, he'd be raised by his father in the colored community and she could never be that child's mother."

"Oh my God, JJ. How horrible. I can't imagine how hard that must've been for that couple." She touched JJ's arm. "What happened?"

"The child was dark and while his mother lay in the hospital after giving birth, the father took him home and raised his son. It wasn't until the child started school and he could keep a secret did he learn who his mother was."

"That's so tragic. To never be able to be a mother to your own flesh and blood. I hope the boy is okay."

"He's fine. Grew up to be a lawyer." He smiled. "He loved his mother very much." JJ turned and pointed to her door. "She lived in this house."

GERI FOSTER

BOOKS BY GERI FOSTER

THE FALCON SECURITIES SERIES
OUT OF THE DARK
WWW.AMAZON.COM/DP/B00CB8GY9K

OUT OF THE SHADOWS
WWW.AMAZON.COM/DP/B00CB4QY8U

OUT OF THE NIGHT
WWW.AMAZON.COM/DP/B00F1F7Q9M

OUT OF THE PAST
WWW.AMAZON.COM/DP/B00JSVTRVU

ACCIDENTAL PLEASURES SERIES

WRONG ROOM
WWW.AMAZON.COM/DP/B00GM9PU94
WRONG BRIDE
WWW.AMAZON.COM/DP/B00NOZMNSU
WRONG PLAN
WWW.AMAZON.COM/DP/B00MO2RFR8
WRONG HOLLY
WWW.AMAZON.COM/DP/B00OBS03M2
WRONG GUY
WWW.AMAZON.COM/DP/B00KK94F6G

ABOUT THE AUTHOR

As long as she can remember, Geri Foster has been a lover of reading and the written words. In the seventh grade she wore out two library cards and had read every book in her age area of the library. After raising a family and saying good-bye to the corporate world, she tried her hand at writing.

Action, intrigue, danger and sultry romance drew her like a magnet. That's why she has no choice but to write action-romance suspense. While she reads every genre under the sun, she's always been drawn to guns, bombs and fighting men. Secrecy and suspense move her to write edgy stories about daring and honorable heroes who manage against all odds to end up with their one true love.

You can contact Geri Foster at geri.foster@att.net.

Made in the USA
Middletown, DE
07 February 2023

24218814R00096